Bosco barked three times at the cardboard box on the counter...

Realization slammed into Elijah. "Bomb!"

He and Tiandra bolted out the askew door and rounded the building just as there was a thunderous boom. Elijah's feet took flight as the impact lifted him into the air.

He landed face-first on the snow-covered lawn and groaned, twisting to see Tiandra next to him. He gripped her arm, and she lifted her head, then scurried to her feet.

Bosco bolted with them as they raced to gain distance from the fiery building. They ran into the copse of evergreens.

Flames stretched high into the evening sky, illuminating the area with a ferocious growling and crackling as they consumed the lodge and surrounding area.

"Are you okay?" Elijah asked.

"I—"

Gunshots pelted the ground near the tree line.

Sharee Stover is a Colorado native transplanted to Nebraska, where she lives with her husband, three children and two dogs. Her mother instilled in her a love of books before Sharee could read, along with the promise "if you can read, you can do anything." When she's not writing, she enjoys time with her family, long walks with her obnoxiously lovable German shepherd and crocheting. Find her at shareestover.com or on Twitter @shareestover.

Books by Sharee Stover

Love Inspired Suspense

Secret Past
Silent Night Suspect
Untraceable Evidence
Grave Christmas Secrets
Cold Case Trail
Tracking Concealed Evidence
Framing the Marshal
Defending the Witness
Seeking Justice

Visit the Author Profile page at LoveInspired.com.

SEEKING JUSTICE

SHAREE STOVER

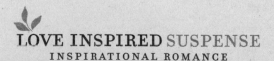

LOVE INSPIRED SUSPENSE
INSPIRATIONAL ROMANCE

LOVE INSPIRED® SUSPENSE

INSPIRATIONAL ROMANCE

Recycling programs for this product may not exist in your area.

ISBN-13: 978-1-335-59909-4

Seeking Justice

Copyright © 2023 by Sharee Stover

For questions and comments about the quality of this book, please contact us at CustomerService@Harlequin.com.

Love Inspired
22 Adelaide St. West, 41st Floor
Toronto, Ontario M5H 4E3, Canada
www.LoveInspired.com

Printed in U.S.A.

Ye shall not fear them:
for the Lord your God he shall fight for you.
—*Deuteronomy* 3:22

Lord Jesus, thank You for the gift of story.
All glory and honor belong to You alone.

ONE

FBI agent Tiandra Daugherty mashed her black combat boot on the gas pedal, fearing she'd stomp a hole through the old pickup's rotting floorboard. The dim beam of the fogged headlights barely illuminated her path through the inky darkness. "Come on," she urged the jalopy.

A familiar and empathetic whine from the backseat reverted her attention to the rearview mirror. Her K-9 Belgian Malinois tilted his head, and she reached back to assure him with one hand. "It's okay, Bosco. We'll be safe soon."

He licked her wrist and whined again, displeased with his safety accommodations. He sat restrained by the expensive dog harness seat belt.

"I'd prefer our SUV too, but that belt will have to do for now."

The K-9 barked his disapproval.

Tiandra focused on the road and gasped. She tugged the wheel, hugging the curve a little too close to the towering rock walls, before skidding back into her lane. "Gotta focus, Bosco." Chest heaving at the near miss, her gaze bounced between the rearview mirror and the hairpin turns of the narrow mountain pass.

South Dakota's beautiful Custer State Park, with its monumental stone, bordered her on both sides. Overhead, a sliver of the moon cast a glow through the Cimmerian atmosphere. Her cell phone vibrated in the cup holder, illuminating the truck's interior. Tiandra didn't need to read the repeated message. The first one had thrown her into action without hesitation.

Get out.

That's all the text had said.
No reason. No justification.
And she didn't need one.
As a seasoned member of the Heartland Fugitive Task Force, acutely aware of high-intensity situations, Tiandra didn't scare easily or question orders. Once she got to the base of operations, she'd find out the reason behind the urgent extraction message.

In the meantime, she contemplated the possibilities. Had HFTF's ten-month investigation and her deep undercover role within the Primo Kings gang finally reached the pinnacle? Worse, had she been made? The truth might set a person free, but in Tiandra's case, her survival depended on a lie. She'd never taken for granted the possibility that someone would discover her true identity, leaving her constantly on high alert. If only she'd had a little more time to finish the Op.

Tiandra tightened her grip on the steering wheel, preparing for Needles Eye Tunnel, a granite formation with the appearance of the eye of a needle that drew tourists from all over the world. But if a person was driving fast at night, the landmark became a death trap. With a clearance of only eight feet, nine inches wide and nine feet, eight inches tall, she had to execute the pass perfectly or risk crashing into the granite stone.

"It's okay, Bosco. Once we get to the meeting location, we'll be safe."

She replayed the previous hour where she'd endured the Kings' raucous party hoping to discover the details for the upcoming drug deal. The task force needed that information to prevent the gang from becoming the largest illegal drug distributors in the Western US. In traditional style, the Kings prematurely celebrated with elaborate festivities, unaware HFTF prepared to take them down in flames.

At least that was the goal until she'd received the extraction text.

Now she had to survive and meet her team.

Defeat weighed on her.

She'd failed to get the information. What if she couldn't return?

She rounded the curve, aiming her truck to thread the needle—as the locals referred to the maneuver—for Needles Eye Tunnel.

"Come on," Tiandra repeated, gripping the steering wheel tighter as she entered the tunnel.

Bosco whined again, always in tune with her disposition.

"We're almost to the turnoff," she assured the K-9, certain he'd read her emotions regardless of her words.

A flash behind her demanded Tiandra's attention. Overly bright headlights filled her rearview mirror, and though she wanted to believe it was just another passerby, Tiandra's instincts said otherwise.

The SUV's engine roared and a slam to the rear bumper of her pickup sent Tiandra swerving dangerously close to the wall.

She recovered from the skid and made it through the passageway.

Outrunning them was impossible, though Tiandra kept her foot pressed to the floorboard. Crags bordered her on both sides. She'd have to fight for control until she came to a clearing.

At last, they exited the stone corridor along the narrow pass with one side plunging to a deep ravine. Tiandra stayed close to the inside wall.

The pursuing vehicle disappeared around the corner.

Then, with a vengeance, the SUV reappeared, engine roaring and announcing its presence.

A second hit to the rear bumper thrust her forward, and she jerked the wheel on the sandy shoulder as she brushed the edge, scraping against the guardrail. Her phone tumbled to the floorboard, out of reach.

The curved mountain road hugged the base of craggy cliffs that loomed overhead beyond her vantage point. She had nowhere to go but down, and that wasn't an option.

Tiandra clung to the steering wheel, one eye fixated ahead, the other on the rearview mirror. The SUV backed slightly, indicating he was toying with his intended kill in a wicked game of predator and prey. Tiandra tried to see the driver, but the darkened windshield and foggy atmosphere prohibited her view.

Dread filled Tiandra as they neared a slender curve. She braced for another hit.

The subsequent slam jolted her small pickup swerving toward the edge.

Tiandra fought to maintain control and almost pulled out of the fishtail, until another impact sent her veering through the guardrail and down the wooded ravine.

Tiandra released the steering wheel, twisting to lean over the headrest and brace her arm over Bosco's body.

They plummeted through the brush in a rapid descent. Glass shattered, and the sickening crash of metal reverberated around her.

The tires bounced against the rocks as they continued to speed toward the dark recesses below.

Screams filled her ears, and in a daze, Tiandra realized the sound came from her.

Her deadly plunge came to a sudden halt when

the pickup collided with a pine tree, emitting a whoosh from the engine and a puff of smoke.

Bosco yelped.

Tiandra groaned and attempted to turn her head, desperate to touch him. "Bos—"

Shooting pain erupted throughout her neck and right shoulder, and she gasped.

She tried reaching for her canine, but the agony in her upper body prevented her from lifting her arm. Still, she was determined to release Bosco from the seat belt, which thankfully had protected him in the crash. She sucked in a breath and strained to twist, spotting his furry form behind her. With an anguished cry, she released his restraint. A click sounded, and she exhaled, exhausted by the effort.

The throbbing intensity coursing up her neck and shoulder roiled nausea through her.

Bosco hopped over the seat and stood beside her. Tiandra fought the spinning sensation. Bile rose in her throat. "I need a second," she whispered.

Warmth trickled down her temple.

His wet tongue swiped at her hand. "Phone—" Tiandra gasped, trying to ask Bosco to retrieve the device from the floorboard. Her words disintegrated with the effort.

Her eyes were heavy.

Through the haze she heard tires screech in the distance, echoing in the ravine.

Tiandra shifted, pushing upright, but the steering wheel pressed hard against her chest, pinning her in a sideways lean.

Darkness closed in around her, but she pried her lids apart, forcing herself to stay awake.

Though she could see no one, footsteps approached, the heavy footfalls speeding through the brush and rocks.

They drew closer.

A gunshot exploded the back window, raining glass on her and Bosco. Tiandra couldn't scream, but she did her best to shield the dog.

Bosco barked wildly, lunging toward the door.

They had plunged to the bottom of the ravine, rushing water burbling nearby. Would the shooter make it down to finish them?

Lord, please protect us, Tiandra prayed with all her mental strength.

Bosco growled and snapped again.

He nestled beside Tiandra, bearing her weight in the awkward position. His velvety fur pressed against her cheek and Bosco's familiar scent comforted her. His whines like pleas for Tiandra to hold on.

Help was coming.

It had to be.

If pain was any indicator, Tiandra was alive. A soft voice dragged her from the quiet depths of darkness. An internal hammer pounded against her skull. She struggled to open her eyes, instead focusing on the woman's heartfelt words.

"Tiandra. Wake up." The voice sounded like ATF agent Skyler Rios. "Come on, sister. We've got work to do."

Definitely Skyler. She never rested.

Tiandra opened one eye, glimpsing the IV taped to her left hand, unsurprised to see her teammate sitting beside her. "I'm not dead."

"Nope." Skyler beamed. "Good morning, sunshine."

"Is it morning?" Tiandra shifted too quickly, instantly regretting the move as a wave of nausea enveloped her.

"No." Skyler chuckled. "It's the middle of the night."

Tiandra pressed her hands on the bed, and Skyler adjusted her pillows, helping her sit upright. A soft glow filled the room, and Tiandra squinted against the light.

"You've been out for a while."

"Aren't visiting hours over?" Tiandra teased. Not that she expected to see the team holding vigil beside her bed, but it was strange not to have them present.

"For normal people." Skyler winked. "Walsh took Bosco home with him a while ago, though."

"I'm glad he's safe." Tiandra's thoughts shot to her partner. "Where is Graham?" She and DEA agent Graham Kenyon had spent nearly a year working undercover in the Primo Kings gang. "He's out flirting with the nursing staff, isn't he?" she half joked.

Skyler's expression sobered. "Let me start with the good news."

"That implies there is bad news." Tiandra tilted her head, anxiety developing within her.

"Bosco and Destiny are becoming besties." Deputy US Marshal Chance Tavalla and his German shepherd, Destiny, were the most recent additions to the team. "Brilliant move securing him in that dog seat belt. Based on the wreckage, he'd have flown out the window without the restraint. He has no injuries but he hasn't stopped whining because he wants to be with you."

"I miss him already." They were never apart for long periods of time. Tiandra's pulse increased.

"You owe your life to Bosco. He shielded you while you were unconscious. Evidence at the scene indicated whoever ran you off the road tried finishing you off. Somehow, Bosco protected you until we got there." Skyler's lengthy explanation was a clear stall tactic.

"Sky, where's Graham?" The silence that followed drove a knife into Tiandra's heart. "No," she gasped, putting a hand to her lips.

"He's not dead," Skyler said.

Tiandra exhaled. "Then what happened?"

Skyler scooted closer. "He sustained serious injuries and hasn't regained consciousness. Graham's in a coma."

"Was he shot?" Tiandra remembered the gunshots fired at her vehicle in the ravine.

"No. The best we can tell, after he texted you to leave the Kings' party, he was en route to the base of operations on his motorcycle when they ran him off the road," Skyler explained. "The same stunt they pulled with you. Did he share anything about the insider with you before that?"

Her partner had only recently indicated there was an insider in the Primo Kings. But Tiandra knew no specifics. "No, he sent the extraction text message, and I bolted." Tiandra's eyes welled with tears. "I want to see him." She attempted to throw off her covers, but the pain had her relenting.

"Slow down, hot rod." Skyler admonished, gripping Tiandra's hand. "The doctor said they'd release you in the morning if you're still doing well."

"Poor Graham. I need to see him for myself." Tiandra pushed up and swung her legs off the bed.

"You can't. Not yet. He's in another hospital under an assumed name."

Confused, Tiandra leaned against the pillows and studied her teammate. "Why? Isn't the case over? If the Kings made Graham, they intended to kill us."

"But if it was their rival, the 29 Locos Cartel, we have a bigger problem," Skyler replied. "We don't know how deep Graham was, if his cover was blown, or what he'd discovered. Until he regains consciousness, we're stuck."

· "Then we have to continue the Op. If the cartel ordered the attack, it means my cover is still good," Tiandra said. "I'll go back in and find where and when the drug deal is going down."

Skyler shook her head. "We're not sure it's safe."

"We can't just stop."

"There's no way you could return without Graham," Skyler argued. "It'll create too many questions and might throw off the deal if they suspect anything."

An idea bloomed and Tiandra said, "No, but we could use a stand-in. A willing participant. Graham's got his own body double."

"Yes!" Skyler jumped to her feet, eyes wide. "His identical twin brother, Elijah!"

Elijah Kenyon leaned against the wall, hand on his Glock. He'd heard movement outside before the stranger rapped on his front door. He tried to peer through the peephole, but something blocked the tiny window, hindering the porch light from displaying his late-night visitor.

Two more knocks.

He glanced at where he'd fallen asleep as he did most nights, sprawled on his couch, watching football game replays. A pizza box lay wide open, exposing the remnants of his dinner on the coffee table alongside the remote control. The television announcer continued narrating plays over the surround sound.

He still wore his Sioux City Police Department uniform and boots. The sixteen-hour shift that involved two high-speed chases with auto thieves had ended in substantial overtime and left him with no sleep the night before.

The clock on the mantle read 03:20.

Another rap on his door demanded his focus. Who would bug him at this hour? He had plenty of enemies. That came with the badge he wore. But most criminals didn't knock before they attacked, he reminded himself.

Elijah sucked in a breath and opened the door.

The woman on the porch stepped back. "Wow, you look just like him." She stood taller and extended her hand, but Elijah's glance traveled to the muscular Belgian Malinois beside her. The dog's stiffened posture offered a silent warning.

Elijah blinked, processing her words. "Beg your pardon?" He lowered his gun-wielding hand, keeping the pistol close to his hip, concealed by the opened door.

"Sorry." She flashed him a one-hundred-watt smile that struck him straight in the knees. "Hello, Elijah, I'm FBI agent Tiandra Daugherty." Her voice was soft, with the slightest Southern accent that coated her words like a dollop of honey. With the hand he'd failed to shake, she reached into her jacket.

Elijah instinctively raised the gun.

She withdrew a leather pouch and held it out for him. Elijah slid the Glock into his hip holster and studied her credentials. FBI agent Tiandra Daugherty. She was legit.

Elijah visually surveyed the woman. A pleasant task considering her willowy frame and beautiful features. No FBI agent he'd ever met looked that good.

"I'm sorry to bother you at this time of night, but it's imperative that I speak with you." She glanced over her shoulder. "Privately."

Elijah followed her gaze to the quiet street bathed in a thin layer of snow accentuated by colorful lights and too many inflatable Christmas characters consuming his neighbor's yard. "Uh, sure, c'mon in." He stepped aside, allowing the agent and her dog to enter before closing the door.

They paused in his entryway, waiting for further instruction.

"Have a seat." He gestured toward the sofa, acutely aware of his awkwardness with women. Elijah leaned against the wall to appear casual. Uncomfortable, he readjusted to stand feet shoulder width apart, arms crossed. If it wasn't his imagination, the dog lifted his chin in a defiant challenge. Elijah diverted his eyes, mindful it was unwise to antagonize the animal by staring him down.

Tiandra and her Malinois made their way around his compact living room. She took a seat on the overstuffed couch and the dog sat at her feet, his focus never leaving Elijah. In the television's ambient light, Elijah spotted the K-9's gray halter and badge on his furry chest, confirming his official capacity.

"Agent Daugherty, what's this about?" Elijah asked, eager to get them out of his house. He flipped on the table lamp.

A somber look passed over her face and he noticed her startling hazel eyes before she glanced away. "Please call me Tiandra," she said, meeting his gaze. "This is K-9 Bosco. We work with your brother, Graham, on the Heartland Fugitive Task Force."

She'd said *work*, as in present tense. If this were a death notification, she'd have used the past tense verb. "Is something wrong?" Elijah's mind whirled with possibilities. "Of course, there is." Why else would the FBI send an agent to talk with him in the middle of the night? He took a step forward, halted by the dog's squared posture. Elijah's gaze traveled from the Malinois to the handler again. "Is Graham hurt?"

"It's okay, Bosco." Tiandra spoke softly while stroking the dog's head, and he dropped to sit beside her. "I'm sorry to bother you at this time—"

"Just say it," Elijah snapped, emotions rising. "I'm a cop, capable of hearing whatever you have to tell me." Horrific thoughts of accidents he'd worked bombarded his mind.

"Graham was injured in a motorcycle accident. It's the reason I'm here."

"Is he okay? What're his injuries? Have you talked to my parents?"

"He's stable, but in a coma. No, we notified you first as per his documented request." She shook her head, a strand of her light brown hair swaying over her shoulder. "Our team wants to meet with you to discuss the details."

"Why?"

"Graham is safe," she assured. "However, there's a pressing issue regarding his safety. Time is of the essence. I'm here to escort you to our base of operations."

"Well, then, let's go. I need to see him."

"Okay. We'll talk on the way," Tiandra said. "You might want to change clothes and grab supplies for an extended stay."

Elijah spun on his heel and hurried to his bedroom. After he'd changed out of his uniform, placed his duty weapon in the lockbox, and secured his personal pistol, he grabbed his go bag and rushed to the living room. "Ready."

He followed Tiandra and Bosco to a black SUV with tinted windows and climbed into the passenger seat while she loaded the dog into the kennel behind him.

Once she'd slid behind the wheel, Elijah asked, "Where exactly are we headed?"

"We're traveling to the airport, where we'll fly to the HFTF BOO. Sorry, base of operations."

"Yes, I'm aware of the acronym," Elijah grumbled.

"—in Keystone, South Dakota," she concluded, starting the engine.

"Negative. I'm not going anywhere until I've seen my brother."

"I understand your worry and concern," she said gently, eyes on the road, "however, Graham's protected and in the best possible care. Once my commander has spoken with you, we'll travel to the hospital." Tiandra gave him a small shrug. "Sorry, Commander Walsh's orders." As though that explained everything.

"I don't work for HFTF, so I'm not obligated to follow his orders," Elijah snapped, instantly regretting his attitude. He swiped a hand over his buzzed hair. "I apologize. I've had little sleep in the past twenty-four hours."

"Allow us to present the full picture." Tiandra's soft tone and tender smile had Elijah averting his gaze. With looks like hers, he'd have to make a special effort to ignore her beauty.

"What hospital is Graham in?" Elijah's brother never shared assignment locations until after the fact, which he understood.

The Belgian Malinois poked his head through a smaller window between them. The opening had a slider door and revealed his kennel behind the seats. Elijah scooted over, startled.

"Sorry, Bosco likes being included." Tiandra chuckled. "Are you an animal guy?"

It seemed there was no alternative answer to that question, especially with the Malinois panting beside his ear. His mother always said honesty was the best policy. "Haven't been around them much. My dad is allergic to just about everything, so we didn't have pets."

Elijah's memories landed on the stray puppy he'd found and begged his parents to keep when he was ten years old. When his father instantly burst into a horrific case of hives, the answer became obvious. They helped Elijah find a home for the puppy, but he'd promised himself he'd never again get attached to an animal.

"Our house was full of kids and critters. I'd feel weird not having a dog." She petted the K-9's ears. "Bosco is more human than canine. If only he talked."

The dog barked twice, and Elijah laughed. "He seems to understand."

"Absolutely."

They drove through town, then aimed for the small airport.

"I don't mean to be a jerk, but I need more information about Graham."

"You deserve all the details." Tiandra sighed. "I'll tell you what I can. We were in South Dakota deep undercover on assignment. Our team's uncertain if our identities were compromised. Graham is in an undisclosed location under a fake identity to maintain his protection detail."

Elijah shifted in the seat, his patience waning. "Look, Agent D—"

"Tiandra," she corrected.

He bit back an annoyed reply, aiming to keep their communication professional. "It's late. Please stop dancing around the issue and update me on the situation."

"The short answer is after ten months, Graham, Bosco, and I infiltrated the Primo Kings gang."

That got Elijah's attention for two reasons. The Kings' nefarious deeds created widespread havoc. The second had him blurting, "You took your dog undercover?" Disbelieving, he watched her facial expression.

"Yes. Many of the gang members have dogs, so that's no big deal. Bosco's strongest skills are in explosion detection, not drugs."

"Doesn't he constantly alert on guns and ammo, then?" Confused, Elijah pushed for a better explanation.

"Not unless he's ordered to search. He's very smart." Tiandra smiled. "We finally made progress with the bigger players. The evening before last, Graham sent me an extraction message. On the way to the base, we were both forced off the road." She focused on the road ahead. "However,

Graham, being on a motorcycle, sustained worse injuries than I did. He's in a coma and hasn't regained consciousness."

Elijah had worked many motorcycle accidents, aware the common description of *donor cycles* was far too accurate. Images flooded him and he shoved them down, tightening his hands into fists. "Do you know who's responsible?"

"No. Graham didn't share intel with me prior to the accident. Since then, our team discovered an unidentified person placed a hit on Graham." She pulled onto the small rural airport road and drove to a hangar, lit by bright LED lights. A white Cessna plane sat on the tarmac. "The bottom line is I need your help to save your brother's life."

"You should've started with that." Elijah threw open his door and added, "I'm in, whatever it takes."

They might not be the best of friends, but nothing trumped family.

TWO

"You want me to impersonate my brother?" Elijah blurted in disbelief, repeating Tiandra's comment.

Since they'd landed and started their drive from the airport, he'd struggled to process the bizzare request. The sunglasses hid Elijah's eyes, and though he appreciated the mega-sized coffee, it did little to produce energy or patience.

"It's doubtful the Kings would spot us out here, but we don't want to chance them following us and endangering the team," Tiandra continued, as if he'd not spoken. "We'll go into details at the BOO." She glanced down. "We also need to gas up, so watch for a service station."

The rising sun peeked over the horizon, illuminating the deserted road, blanketed by freshly fallen snow and evergreens that dotted the landscape. "I've never seen this side of South Dakota."

Tiandra nodded. "It's gorgeous."

"Look, I'm terrible at small talk." Elijah spotted a sign for a familiar named gas station and pointed out the window. "Next exit."

"Hmm. I'd prefer to stay off the main thoroughfare." She glanced at the gauges again. "However, running out of gas in the middle of nowhere is unwise." Tiandra pulled off the road and onto the highway leading to Rapid City. "We'll hit the first gas station we see, then backtrack."

Within minutes, they located a smaller service station and Elijah fueled the SUV while Tiandra ran inside to use the restroom. He had replaced the pump when she came hurrying out. "Get in."

Wordlessly, he obeyed the instructions as Tiandra slid behind the wheel and put the vehicle into motion, taking several turns in what seemed like random directions.

"What was that all about?" Elijah asked, once they merged onto the highway they'd departed.

"I recognized a woman in there. She's hung around the Kings' parties. I don't think she saw me. At least I hope not."

Elijah glanced out the side mirror. "There's no one following us."

Tiandra's demeanor said she was unconvinced. They drove beneath a cement underpass, and she jerked the wheel, taking them down into the ditch.

She regained control and returned to the pavement.

Elijah twisted in his seat to see what Tiandra had swerved to avoid. Someone had strewn a line of spikes resembling stop sticks across the road. Two black pickups sped toward them. "We have company."

"I see them."

The Malinois popped his furry head between them. "Bosco, down!"

He disappeared into his kennel.

"They've got long guns." Elijah referred to the rifles that materialized from the passenger-side windows, aimed in their direction.

A barrage of bullets pelting the SUV drowned out Tiandra's order, "Get down!"

The trucks moved to flank them on both sides and Elijah reached for his Glock. "We're surrounded."

"There's a curve coming up. The street narrows so they can't stay fringed."

Another bombardment of firepower sent Elijah ducking in his seat, eyes on the mirror. "I need to return fire."

"Hold off."

They approached the bend, and she accelerated.

Elijah caught sight of the guns aimed at the side windows. "Get down!"

Tiandra ducked just as the shattering glass rained on them. The sound of the wind whipping through the vehicle was deafening. She jerked the wheel to the right, swiping the truck on Elijah's side. The driver's attempted recovery sent the SUV skidding on the icy shoulder.

The other truck came within inches on Tiandra's side, and the passenger reached into the SUV, grabbing the steering wheel.

Elijah aimed, but before he fired, Bosco lunged for the intruder, clamping his jaws on the attacker's arm.

The man screamed and released the steering wheel, yanking back his arm. Tiandra slammed on the brakes. The truck beside her barreled ahead, crashing into the rocky wall edge.

Tiandra accelerated. "Good job, Bosco!"

Elijah gaped. "He's amazing."

"Yes, he is."

Panting happily, Bosco shifted to the backseat.

"We need to get somewhere safe and make sure he's not showered in glass."

Elijah glanced at the rearview mirror. "There's no sign of our attackers."

"Okay, I'm getting off this road. There's a small rock formation on the hill nearby that'll provide cover and a vantage point to ensure they're not following." Tiandra took a turn on a narrow path, canopied by snow-laden evergreens. She pulled around a massive boulders and parked. With the engine running, she threw open her door, then jumped out and released Bosco.

Elijah rounded the vehicle, watching the road. "Clear so far."

"Good." Tiandra retrieved a blanket from the back and together they swept the glass to the side and put the cover down for Bosco.

"He's not injured, is he?" Elijah worried for the brave creature.

"Nope. Bosco's bulletproof with a cat's nine lives." Tiandra knelt next to him, running her hands through his short fur. The dog licked her cheek, and she hugged his neck. "We're cool."

They were quite the team.

"Should we keep going?" Elijah asked once he'd ensured no one had followed them.

"Yes. I'll update the team and explain our delay. I want to take a different path to the BOO." Tiandra lifted her phone, and Elijah listened as she made the call.

He marveled at the steadiness of her voice and nonplussed response after the life-threatening attack they'd narrowly survived. Tiandra's bravery and stamina amazed him. No wonder the Heartland Fugitive Task Force had recruited her. Elijah studied the FBI agent, concluding that working with Tiandra Daugherty was no hardship.

Tiandra surveyed Elijah, sitting across from her in the BOO meeting room, contemplating the uncanny similarities between him and Graham. Both had short sandy blond hair and stunning gray-blue eyes. Their muscular builds were housed in six-foot-one-inch athletic frames. Aside from their identical physical appearance, they also had the same mannerisms and voice inflections. Elijah was a perfect double for Graham, but she reminded herself they were different men. Though Elijah, like the task force, had accepted the daily risks as part of his chosen profession, he wasn't an HFTF member.

Her gaze traveled the room, lingering on each

person. They were as much Tiandra's family as the blood-related six sisters and four brothers she'd grown up with. She'd do anything to protect her fellow team members. They fought and loved fiercely, just like the Daugherty clan. Her thoughts stilled when she recalled that Meghan, her oldest sibling, held Tiandra responsible for their youngest sister Anissa's death. Tiandra shook off the memory. Now wasn't the time.

"I think Elijah impersonating Graham is our best shot," Tiandra said. Still, she'd lived enough in the real world to understand that the kind of loyalty among the Daughertys wasn't true of every family. Was it fair to ask Elijah for this sacrifice? For the first time, she looked past the goal of taking down the Primo Kings. Maybe having Elijah imitate Graham was unwise. But if not, where would they turn?

"I'll do my best to pull off the impersonating role, but my brother and I are very different," Elijah said, interrupting her internal debate. "Will the Kings notice?"

Stubborn. Difficult. Tiandra bit her lip. *Actually, you're not.* She fought back a grin.

"Solid point," Deputy US Marshal Riker Kastell interjected. "Graham went radio silent toward the end. Other than stating he'd discovered an insider working for the Kings and their rival, the 29 Locos Cartel, we have no idea what he'd found or who he'd talked to."

"We're not walking away from this now," Tiandra argued, reengaged in the conversation. "We've worked too hard to takedown the Kings."

"If you're compromised, you're dead before you walk in the door," Skyler said.

Tiandra pinned her teammate with a glare. Why wasn't she backing the cause? "That's an assumption. We don't know who ordered the hit on Graham."

"Or who tried to kill you," Skyler contended.

"Everyone, stop and breathe." Commander Beckham Walsh's booming voice silenced the room. "I appreciate what you all bring to this argument and your points are all equally valuable. However, my biggest concern is protecting my team."

Tiandra opened her mouth to argue, but Walsh's piercing gaze had her clamping it shut. He persisted, "Without knowing who ordered the hit on Graham, we cannot assume Tiandra and Elijah are safe to resume their undercover roles within the Kings."

"Which is why we must continue," Tiandra blurted out, unable to contain the comment. She wouldn't give up this case. "Y'all need to remember, if the Kings receive and distribute those drugs cut with Fentanyl, or something worse, we're responsible for multiple casualties."

"We understand your passion for stopping the gang," Skyler replied softly.

A retaliatory remark lingered on Tiandra's lips, dcfused by the kindness in her friend's eyes.

Elijah tilted his head, sporting a quizzical expression as he shifted his attention to Tiandra.

"My baby sister Anissa would've been twenty-two this year," Tiandra explained. "She died of a Fentanyl overdose, thanks to the Kings." She averted her gaze. "Commander, with all due respect, I cannot walk away from this. Someone else's sister, brother, mother, or father will fall into the same fate as Anissa. Please. Let's finish this. The drug deal should happen within the next week or so. We're so close." Tiandra sighed. "C'mon, guys. We could wrap this case up with a big bow for Christmas."

"That's a lofty goal considering Christmas is less than two weeks away," Skyler said.

"We don't yet have a date or time," Riker explained to Elijah. "If the Kings take possession of the drugs, they'll become the biggest distributor in the Western US."

"And Graham remains in danger," Chance inserted. "Whoever ordered the hit on his life won't give up. That leaves Graham and Elijah in a killer's target. They share a face."

Eliana Kastell, Riker's wife, and the team's tech expert, peered up from her computer. "I'll keep working on the intel. We found out about the hit. We'll find out who ordered it too."

Tiandra shot her a grateful look.

"I'm no victim and neither is Graham. We'll tackle this with an offensive approach," Elijah said, sitting up straighter in his chair. "How fast can you get me up to speed on the case specifics?"

Bosco moved to Elijah, glancing up expectantly, tail thumping.

He smiled and stroked the dog's head. "Hey, buddy."

Tiandra and Skyler shared a knowing glance. Elijah had the same passion as Graham when he spoke, but his willingness to acknowledge Bosco separated them. Graham wasn't much of a dog lover. He preferred flirting with women he encountered. A trait Tiandra had noticed Elijah didn't imitate.

"If Elijah doesn't show up with Tiandra, it'll create suspicion," Skyler conceded.

Walsh sighed, running a hand over his head. "Tiandra, take the lead and find out when the deal will go down. However…" He paused for several seconds, commanding everyone's attention. "If you get even a frog's hair of a hint that either of your covers are compromised, or that the hit came from the Kings, abort mission. Immediately."

"Roger that." Tiandra exhaled relief and glanced at her undercover phone. "Penny Benton is texting." She flicked her gaze at Elijah. "She's the girlfriend of Mikko Stefanov. We've bonded over the shared pain of losing a sibling."

"Mikko is the leader of the Kings?" Elijah

walked to the evidence board and pointed to the man's latest mug shot, surrounded by surveillance pictures.

Grateful Elijah didn't dwell on the lost sibling comment, Tiandra replied, "Yes."

"He's a dirtbag gang member from a big inner city?" Elijah asked.

"Actually, he's the only son of a Nebraska farmer," Riker inserted. "Apparently the father passed some time ago, leaving everything to Mikko aka Michael, who lost the land in his climb to the drug ladder top."

"That's not what I expected." Elijah leaned against the wall, arms crossed. "How does Penny fit into all of this? Is she forthcoming about Mikko's criminal actions?"

"Not yet. We're building trust. Besides his usual henchmen, Vito and Orlando, she's the closest one to him and very protective." Tiandra scrolled through the texts. "Good news. She's asking where I am."

"If Mikko ordered the hit, surely Penny would know," Skyler replied.

"Or she's spying for Mikko to see if Tiandra survived," Chance argued.

"Doubtful. Her messages are normal ramblings and chitchat," Tiandra said. "Nothing to indicate she's got a clue what happened after I left the party."

"I agree," Eliana chimed in. "I'm monitoring the communications to Tiandra's and Graham's cell phones and it's all typical."

"Hmm, sounds as though the Kings aren't the ones who ordered the hit," Elijah contended.

Riker jumped into the discussion. "That gives Elijah something to lead with." He addressed Elijah. "Go in there hotter than an angry hornet and demand answers to the accident."

"Yeah," Chance agreed. "Mikko's response will tell us everything we need to know."

"On second thought, if we're wrong and Mikko's responsible for the hit, Elijah's a dead man walking," Riker replied.

"Dude." Chance shook his head.

"Just keeping it real." Riker's candid speech left little room for niceties.

"Graham's fighting for his life in the hospital." Elijah's posture remained strong, but Tiandra caught the quiver in his voice. His Adam's apple bobbed as he swallowed hard. "I'll fight for his life out here."

"We're in the battle with you. The Heartland Fugitive Task Force is a family too. In this mission, you've become one of us," Walsh said. "I've already spoken with your chief and arranged a leave of absence."

"You did?" Elijah walked to the table and dropped into a chair. "How?"

"Walsh knows everyone," Skyler said with a wink.

"I requested you train with us," Walsh explained.

"Remember, this is a confidential operation. Graham is safe, and we're closely monitoring him."

"Thank you." Elijah's whispered reply was barely audible.

Something Tiandra couldn't quite define passed in his expression.

"I have an off-topic question," Elijah said. "Doesn't your team hunt fugitives? How does that fit into this mission?"

"The Kings harbor several fugitives on the FBI's Most Wanted List," Walsh said. "When we caught onto their plans for the drugs, we combined goals, creating a single operation."

"It'll be a BOGO arrest," Skyler added.

Elijah's forehead creased in confusion.

"Buy one, get one," Eliana explained. "Two for the price of one."

Elijah nodded. "Smart."

"It was Graham's idea," Tiandra said.

"All right, team, let's work out the nitty-gritty details," Walsh said.

After several minutes of logistics discussion, the group dispersed to their stations, filling the room with activity.

Elijah got to his feet and returned to study the evidence board covered with mug shots and crime scene photos of Tiandra's pickup truck crash and Graham's mangled motorcycle.

Tiandra found it impossible to look at Elijah and not see his brother. But Graham's overwhelming confidence and tendancy to exude all his qualifications contrasted with Elijah's quiet strength. His humble attitude spoke louder than words.

Tiandra approached him. "We're asking a lot." Elijah didn't turn around, so she continued, "You've got the training and skills. We need to convince the Kings you're Graham."

"Or I'll fail and get us both killed."

Tiandra didn't respond.

She couldn't. They played a tough game with smoke-and-mirror ruses, convincing criminals of their identities. But once they had the meeting location, HFTF would step in and make the arrests. "I have no doubt you can do this."

"Who said I couldn't?" He hesitated in front of the accident scene picture with Graham's motorcycle twisted around a massive tree trunk. "Excuse me." He spun on his heel and exited the room.

Bosco sidled up to her, and Tiandra squatted to pet him. "Buddy, I need you to turn on the charm."

He quirked a furry brow as if to say, *I never turned it off.*

Tiandra chuckled, then studied the board, pondering Graham's behavior prior to the text message. Why hadn't he shared intel? Without it, he'd left them all in a quandary of unknowns that might prove deadly. They were dealing with a faceless enemy who wanted Graham dead and would willingly include needless casualties.

Except the danger wasn't what bothered her.

Rather, she contemplated Graham's meeting several weeks prior with Walsh. He'd requested Tiandra's transfer out of the case. The betraying wound was a blow to her heart and ego. She and Bosco were great partners, and they'd proven their capabilities. Worse, she'd considered Graham a friend.

They'd worked in sync until he'd pushed her away and refused to share intel, treating her like a civilian rather than an equal. And what the group hadn't discussed, but Tiandra wondered, was whether Graham was compromised. And if he was, were they throwing Elijah to the Kings mercilessly?

THREE

Elijah leaned against the brick wall of the old building and inhaled deeply. Between lack of sleep and the information overload the task force dumped on him in the briefing, he was close to screaming or punching someone. Worse, when the lightbulb of recognition lit up regarding Tiandra Daugherty, he had to control his response.

She wasn't just an FBI agent. If he'd correctly deciphered Graham's comments about being attracted to a woman he worked with, Tiandra was that person. Though Graham had never mentioned her by name, the pieces started falling into place, making Tiandra off-limits.

Guilt and annoyance warred within him. He couldn't view her as anything more than a coworker. Brothers didn't backstab one another over women. However, based on the way the team talked and Tiandra's actions, it appeared Graham never shared his feelings. Or perhaps that was Elijah's wishful thinking. Not that the situation surprised him.

The siblings' complicated relationship wove a web of love and resentment, dragging them into an endless tug-of-war game. No matter what Elijah did, Graham did it better. And no amount of time and distance changed that.

Now these strangers assumed that because Elijah and Graham shared physical features, they were the same man.

And they couldn't be more wrong.

Graham was the star DEA agent with the elite Heartland Fugitive Task Force. His life rested in the hands of his second-best, small-town cop twin. If Elijah failed to convince the Kings... No, now wasn't the time for those defeatist thoughts. He'd finish the Op and find his brother's hired assassin.

Elijah sucked in a fortifying breath, embracing his role as live bait set to lure the killer.

No problem. He groaned, closing his eyes, and scrubbed his palms over his hair. Face raised upward, he prayed, *Lord, give me the confidence and skills needed to be my brother's imposter. Help us find and arrest whoever is out to hurt Graham. Show me what to do.*

He had to protect Graham and bring down the criminal.

Or die trying.

Elijah turned, fleeing the familiar voice of doubt vying for his thoughts again. He entered the empty foyer. The team had probably resumed their discussion. Why wouldn't they? He wasn't a member, so they had no reason to wait on him.

He trudged to the room where they'd collaborated earlier and found them deep in conversation. Elijah hesitated near the door, though they continued talking.

No. They were praying.

He'd never seen a group like this one.

After the collective "Amen," Commander Walsh lifted his head, spotting Elijah and waved him inside. "Elijah, we've received word about Graham."

He froze in place.

"His condition has declined." Compassion hung in Skyler's tone. "The next few hours are critical."

"I need to see him." Elijah hurried in.

"Agreed," Walsh replied. "With the stipulation that you and Tiandra do so in disguise."

"We've taken extreme precautions to protect and conceal Graham's identity," Riker said. "We don't want anyone recognizing the two of you."

Chance stood. "Come with me."

Elijah followed the deputy marshal to a back room. A latex nose and colored contacts along with a wig and mustache—that appeared surprisingly natural—sat atop a table. Their premeditated planning touched Elijah.

By the time he and Chance completed the transformation, Elijah didn't recognize himself.

He returned to where the rest of the team had assembled.

Skyler looked up and grinned. "Well done."

Walsh nodded. "I'll say."

Bosco tilted his head and barked, eliciting a collective chuckle from the group.

"Elijah, you look like a whole new man. Great work, Chance." Tiandra stood. "We should get going." She ushered him out the door, Bosco trotting along.

Confused by her abruptness and lack of disguise, he slid into the SUV passenger seat wordlessly.

Once they were on the road, Tiandra aimed for the airport again. "Remember, no matter what he looks like, remain composed."

"I've worked in undercover capacities before."

"Yeah, but this is different." Tiandra's voice softened. "This life isn't for everyone. I'm not sure I'd sign up for a dangerous mission if I were you."

"It's not about me." Elijah settled in the seat. "Wouldn't you do the same to save your brother?"

Her quirked brow had him regretting his words. She'd told him about her sister's death. *Nice, big mouth.*

"Absolutely. I'll do whatever it takes to protect any of the ten of them."

Elijah gaped. "You have ten siblings?"

"Yep, four brothers and six sisters." She smiled. "Without telling my age, I'm somewhere in the middle on the older side of the group."

"Wow." That revelation was unexpected. Though he wanted to ask her a hundred questions, maintaining a professional distance with Tiandra was imperative. The less he knew about her, the better.

The conversation dwindled, and until Tiandra touched his arm, startling him awake, Elijah didn't realize he'd fallen asleep. He bolted upright in his seat, the belt tightening against his torso.

"We're here."

He spotted the same white Cessna plane. "Sorry, I didn't mean to doze on you."

"Don't apologize. Take the opportunities when you can. You won't get much sleep once we're with the Kings."

They exited the SUV and boarded the plane. Elijah took a window seat, opting to stare outside rather than talk.

Impersonating Graham rubbed salt in the sibling rivalry wound. If HFTF had recruited him for his skills and abilities, he wouldn't feel the sting of walking in his brother's shadow.

They had no idea what they weren't getting in Elijah. Worse, they'd sent a beautiful FBI agent to partner with him. As ridiculous as it sounded, that picked at old emotional scars from the past, reminding him that another woman had preferred Graham but settled for him.

When the plane made its descent and touchdown, Elijah couldn't wait to exit the aircraft. Consumed by his thoughts, he hadn't noticed Tiandra's absence. Now, as she walked toward him, her disguise surprised him. She'd changed into a dress and heels. She also wore a dark wig that trailed down her back and blue contact lenses, hiding her hazel eyes.

"What do you think?" She grinned.

You're gorgeous. "Definitely different." Her smile faltered, and he felt like a complete jerk. "I mean, it's nice. You look great." But the damage was done.

"I just can't look like myself," she mumbled, turning to speak with the man at the foot of the steps. "Bring Bosco to the meet location and wait for me," she instructed the stranger, not bothering to introduce Elijah. Then to Bosco, "I'll see you soon, buddy."

They got into a compact car located on the tarmac. Tiandra drove the short commute to the Clearwater, Florida, hospital, and they made small talk about the scenery and traffic.

Finally, she parked in the hospital garage and faced him. "Now remember, we're not here to see Graham. He's under an assumed name. I'll speak to the nurse. Got it?"

"Affirmative." Elijah wondered about Graham's cover identity, but he didn't press for the information.

They walked at a clipped pace through the hospital, all the while Elijah worrying someone would realize they wore disguises. To his relief, no one questioned them.

When they reached the secured floor, Tiandra spoke to a nurse who provided a badge and released the locked doors. They proceeded along a hallway to where two marshals stood guard.

With a single nod, Tiandra entered the room, Elijah behind her. He stopped dead in his tracks at the sight of his barely recognizable twin lying in the bed. Bruises covered Graham's swollen and battered face, but it was him. No doubt.

Everything within Elijah was certain of that.

Tiandra stepped aside, giving Elijah space to approach the bedside. Monitors and medical machines lit up the room in a variety of colors and sounds. A tube from Graham's mouth led to the ventilator hissing a soft rhythm. A cast enveloped Graham's left arm, hanging suspended from a rod and thick wire. Likewise, a cast from hip to foot encased his right leg.

Righteous anger and sorrow mingled within Elijah.

"I'll give you some privacy." Tiandra exited the room.

Unable to tear his eyes from Graham, Elijah didn't respond. The visual proof of his brother's horrific injuries opened a floodgate of tumultuous emotions. What if he never got to talk to him again? What if they never found a way to get past the rivalry that plagued their relationship from birth? What if it was too late?

"G, this is quite the set-up, bro. You always were an overachiever," Elijah quipped, the bad joke falling flat. Tears stung his eyes, but he refused to let them fall. Not yet. If his brother didn't survive, he'd grieve then. "You know I'm not you." He gave a bitter laugh. "You'd jump on that comment in a heartbeat if you were conscious."

Elijah hung his head and sent up a silent prayer of healing for his twin.

He extended a hand to touch Graham's face, then withdrew before making contact. "You keep fighting, bro. I'll find who did this and make sure they pay. I am my brother's keeper."

The door swung open, and Tiandra entered. "I'm sorry to rush you, but it's dangerous for us to be here."

Elijah walked past her. "I'm ready."

If Tiandra and Elijah didn't expose the drug deal date and location, ten months of deep undercover was lost. And if they died trying, Graham might never be safe again. The combination of high stakes kept them on their toes and left Tiandra leaning heavily on God.

Her mother would say that was exactly where she needed to be. The tender reminder lifted the corner of her lips. The sun hovered low in the sky, like a visual gesture of God's sovereignty over the case. *Lord, I can't do this without You.*

Bosco snored softly in the SUV's backseat, exhausted from the extensive travel to and from Florida. Tiandra turned onto the highway, the Rapid City airport in her rearview mirror.

Exhaustion weakened her body and pain racked her from her still-healing injuries. Though she'd never confess that aloud. Especially after visiting Graham. His critical condition had hardened her resolve to find the attacker, and based on Elijah's demeanor, his too. She prayed it wasn't the last time they'd see Graham alive.

Yet his betrayal lingered, confusing her emotions. He'd withheld intel, not just from her, but from the entire team. She'd known Graham for a decade and had never once considered he'd compromise an investigation.

Until now.

Tiandra's mother would say she'd allowed her anger to develop into a bitter root in her heart. And she'd be correct. However, Tiandra couldn't deny witnessing her incapacitated partner had chipped away the rough edges.

"How did your team find you in time?" Elijah's question intruded on her ruminations.

"What?" Tiandra asked.

"After the accident."

"Oh, the GPS on my cell phone."

Elijah only nodded.

A low rumble emitted from where he sat, and she flicked a glance his way.

He shrugged. "Sorry, guess I'm hungry." Elijah's adorable, boyish expression made her smile.

Adorable? No, she told herself. He was a coworker. Nothing more. She focused hard on the road. "I can't remember the last time I ate a full meal," she said, diverting her wandering thoughts. "We have a long drive ahead of us. Let's stop and grab something."

"What about staying incognito?"

They'd changed into street clothes, tossing their disguises in a trash bin before leaving the airport.

Tiandra considered her jeans and leather jacket. "Hmm, good point. I'd say we'll just have to be extra careful. Guess we should've held on to them a little longer. Although truthfully, I couldn't get out of that dress fast enough."

"Really?" He grinned. "Not into getting all dolled up?"

"No." Tiandra snorted. "Even before I went undercover with rub-on tattoos, combat boots, and jeans, that wasn't my style. I'm grateful Skyler pulled it together for me."

"She did a great job. You looked amazing." Elijah cleared his throat. "I mean… This outfit also suits you well."

Warmth filled her face, surprising Tiandra. Why did his compliment feel like a ray of sunshine in the middle of a rainy day? "So, what're you hungry for?" she asked, desperate to refocus the discussion elsewhere.

"I'm not picky."

"Me either. I'll pull over at the first drive-thru."

Christmas carols played over the radio, filling the car with an out-of-place joyfulness.

"Did you recognize anyone in the trucks that tried to take us out earlier?"

"No," Tiandra said. "Definitely not the Kings. They prefer sleek rides to four-by-four pickups."

Grateful they were talking about the case again, she added, "The woman at the convenience store was familiar, but we've never interacted. I'm assuming she's a wannabe gang member girlfriend."

"Are there many of them hanging around?"

"Yeah, especially when there are parties like the most recent shindig." Tiandra considered the events. "However, I won't dismiss the timing."

"I can't figure out how they came after us so quickly."

"That part isn't a surprise. Whoever hired the hit on Graham is horribly talented in tracking his prey."

"You make them sound like animals."

"If a killer sees weakness, he pounces. They're all alike. The Kings are the same way. And this deal is essential to their survival."

"The good news is, the assassin believes I am Graham."

"Exactly. It's probably the single reason Walsh allowed us to continue this Op." She spotted a sign for a familiar restaurant. "There's a mom-and-pop diner off the next exit. A total hole in the wall."

"Works for me."

Tiandra pulled into the building's crumbling parking lot.

"You weren't kidding." Elijah edged closer to the windshield, peering out. "*A hole in the wall* is a generous description. Are you sure this place is open?"

"Yep. And it serves the best burgers you've ever had." She paused. "On second thought, I can't take in Bosco."

"I'll grab a to-go order and we'll eat in the SUV," he suggested. "What do you recommend?" Elijah shot a wary glance at the restaurant.

"Everything."

"Okay, then." He laughed. "I'll be right back."

"Please grab a plain burger for Bosco." She reached for her purse, and he waved her off.

"I got this." Elijah exited the vehicle and disappeared through the single door, wafting the aroma of grilled meat to her.

Tiandra got out and released Bosco. "Come on. Let's take a quick break."

The dog peeked at her and emitted a lazy yawn, stretching out his legs.

"Take your time," she teased.

Bosco hopped off the seat and out of the vehicle. Tiandra started to snap on his leash, then decided against it. "Stick close, buddy."

A slight wag of his tail confirmed Bosco's cooperation.

They perused the parking lot covered in a thin layer of snow.

No passersby appeared on the road and a cold winter breeze fluttered her hair.

"Bosco, what do we do now?"

The Malinois ignored her, intent on his exploration mission.

Tiandra mentally flipped through her options, recalling Walsh's counteroffer. When Elijah had gone outside at the BOO, Walsh had suggested Tiandra return to the Kings and claim Graham had abandoned her. She could play up the scene by accusing him of infidelity and hope to find the drug deal location. But that meant going in alone.

Though she'd not expressed her rejection of Walsh's idea, Tiandra did nothing alone.

She always had Bosco, but an Op was different. It required her to be on guard, anticipating an attack without backup.

If the Kings suspected her real identity, they'd kill her before she could call for help.

Tiandra's greatest skill was her ability to be a team player. Her worst was her fear of working solo. In the decade she'd spent with HFTF, she'd never admitted that because they were all about teamwork. At the BOO, Tiandra had played that up in the discussion, emphasizing the need for Elijah to impersonate Graham because of the high stakes.

She inhaled deeply. *God grant us the wisdom and opportunity to finish this Op. For Anissa and Graham. As well as for future victims the Kings' drugs would claim.*

Elijah's unwavering resolve to fight and protect Graham proved what her father had always said.

Soldiers are made. Warriors are born.

Her phone rang, startling Tiandra.

"Any change?" Walsh asked in greeting. The man never started with *hello*.

"No. He looks pretty bad, though, boss."

Walsh sighed. "And Elijah?"

"I think seeing his brother in that state was a shock, but it seemed to boost his intentions. He's totally in."

"Okay. Head to the BOO ASAP to formulate our POA."

"Roger that." She disconnected, grinning at Walsh's overuse of acronyms. The plan of action was simple. Return to the Kings' hideout and stay alive while discovering the drug deal date, time, and location.

Elijah exited the restaurant, the open door again sending delicious aromas in her direction. He carried a massive plastic bag with both hands. "Ready?"

"Yep." She used the key fob to unlock the SUV, keeping one eye on Bosco who had meandered to the edge of the pavement to investigate dead foliage. At her whistle, he trotted obediently to her side.

Elijah placed the large bag inside the vehicle and they loaded up.

"Let's get off the main road." Tiandra started the engine. "We'll head to higher ground."

She drove to a spot that overlooked the valley below and parked. Elijah retrieved the food while

Tiandra withdrew a bottled water and a portable dog bowl from her large purse.

"Wow, that's the first time I've seen a woman carry something like that in her purse," Elijah teased.

"I always come prepared." She winked and poured water into the bowl, setting it down on the floorboard for Bosco, who lapped it greedily.

"Mind if I give thanks?"

Pleasantly surprised, she bowed her head while he prayed over the meal. She broke apart Bosco's massive plain hamburger and placed it on the box lid. Then returned to her own lunch.

Elijah had already taken a bite of his burger and was enthusiastically chewing.

"Good?" She laughed.

He nodded, shoving a steak fry into his mouth.

Tiandra bit into the delicious meat, bread, and sauce combination. "Comfort food."

Their accommodations were uncomfortable but that didn't prevent them from relishing the meal in record time.

Tiandra shoved her trash into the bag. "I need a nap now."

The Malinois barked.

"Does that mean he agrees?" Elijah chuckled.

"I wish," Tiandra groaned. "He needs a few moments of privacy." She exited and released Bosco.

Elijah joined them at the edge of the trees, the dog trotting ahead to sniff the area.

A revving engine caught her attention, and she glanced past Elijah. A car sped along the winding road, driving too fast in their direction.

"Let's go!" Tiandra whistled for Bosco.

The trio started for the SUV, but the oncoming vehicle reached it first and skidded to a stop. The illegally tinted passenger window lowered, and a gun muzzle emerged.

Bosco barked and tackled Tiandra to the ground.

She landed behind a boulder in the icy snow with an *oomph*, the air whooshing from her lungs.

Gunfire emitted around them, pulverizing the SUV.

FOUR

Bosco bolted over them, darting in and out of the tree line in zigzag moves. Twilight provided shadowed cover where Elijah lay flattened on the ground beside Tiandra. They'd shoot the dog! Horrified, Elijah yelled, "What's he doing?"

Gunshots whipped past them, aimed toward the K-9's abrupt exit.

"Distracting them." Tiandra pushed into a crouched position, shielded behind the massive stone.

Then, as quickly as it began, the gunfire ended.

Elijah peered over the boulder, spotting a truck coming up the road. The car sped away, the tires squealing on the asphalt before it disappeared around the curve. The truck drove past without stopping.

Tiandra gave a shrill whistle and Bosco bounded from the evergreen branches.

"Is he okay?"

"Yes." She swept her hand over the dog, inspecting his fur. "Not a mark on him. Good job, buddy!"

He dropped to a sit, tail swishing the snowy ground, absorbing his partner's praise.

"You're right. He's part cat." Elijah stood and helped Tiandra to her feet. "How many lives is that?"

"I lost count years ago. Let's get out of here."

The trio returned to the SUV, pockmarked by multiple bullet holes and a flat tire. "Great," Tiandra groaned.

"No problem." Elijah went to work pulling out the jack and spare tire while Tiandra updated the task force.

She disconnected as Elijah tightened the last lug nut and jumped to his feet.

"That's the fastest tire changing I've ever witnessed."

He bowed, earning him a chuckle.

"This is going to be a cold ride." Tiandra gestured to the blown-out windows.

"Hold on." Elijah removed his jacket, placing it on the backseat for Bosco, who wasted no time in curling up on it.

"You don't have to do that."

"Not a problem." Elijah smiled. "The frosty air will keep me alert."

"Thank you." She touched his forearm.

Elijah fought not to show his reaction, but her touch sent a shock through him. "We'd better scoot."

They loaded up and Tiandra started the engine, keeping the headlights off, and turned onto the road.

"Now where to?"

"The BOO. I need supplies before we go into the Kings' lair."

For the first time, Elijah noticed Tiandra's ripped sleeve and the crimson spot on her neck. She didn't complain, simply kept driving as though it was no issue. The woman was a steel interior wrapped in a gorgeous exterior.

Knock it off. His internal reprimand had Elijah focusing on the scenery outside the window. Nothing had changed. Graham's feelings for Tiandra meant she was off-limits.

Determined to focus on the job, he asked, "Why'd the shooter just take off like that?"

"My guess is the impromptu truck that drove by interrupted their plans."

"Did they follow us from the airport?"

"Doubtful. I watched for tails. Somehow, they're keeping up with our location." Tiandra whipped the car into a U-turn, heading in the opposite direction.

"Did I miss something?"

"Use my phone and call Walsh on speakerphone, please."

Elijah did as she asked. The line rang once before Walsh's baritone voice answered. "What's wrong?"

"Transfer to burner."

"Roger that."

Tiandra jerked a chin toward her large purse. "Inside there's a burner flip phone. Turn it on and answer when it rings."

"My mom threatened our lives if we got into her purse."

She chuckled. "Normally I'd say that's accurate, but today's a special occasion."

With the trepidation of handling a poisonous snake, he withdrew the device, which rang as soon as he powered it on. "Hello?"

"What's happened?" Walsh continued as though there'd been no break in the conversation.

"The BOO is a bad idea," Tiandra responded. "Not sure if they're tracing my cell. We didn't have issues in Florida, but now we're back to dodging killers."

"Agreed." Elijah recognized Riker's voice.

"If the killer suspects I'm impersonating Graham, he's in danger too," Elijah said.

"We'll ramp up his protection detail," Skyler replied.

"But with all the attacks, I'd say the ruse is working," Chance added.

"Can you meet us at the old grain store for a vehicle swap?" Tiandra asked.

"Yep," Riker answered. "On our way."

"We'll need supplies," Tiandra said, all business. "Not sure when we'll get the next in-person meeting."

"On it," Skyler replied.

"See you in twenty." Riker ended the call.

Elijah set the phone on the console between them. "Okay, now what?"

"We embrace our roles."

"We talked some at the BOO, but tell me more

details about what my brother did, how he acted, et cetera."

"The key to undercover identities is intertwining your normal behaviors or personality within the character. Makes it easier than trying to act out a completely different individual."

"Graham and I aren't the same person." How much of Tiandra was her cover versus her real persona? Elijah visually surveyed her, dressed in dark jeans, a leather jacket, and combat boots with her brown hair pulled into a severe ponytail. Though they'd just fought for their lives, her appearance remained unmarred. Intrigued and battling his curiosity, he forced himself to focus on the case. "Did Graham stay true to his dislike of the outdoors?"

Tiandra chuckled. "Um, yeah. He's definitely not into roughing it. He hates the hideout where we've crashed with the gang."

They stayed in the same house, together?

As though sensing his unease, Tiandra clarified, "We have our own rooms and whenever possible, we make excuses to lodge elsewhere. It's hard to be this alternative personality all the time, always worried someone will kill you in the middle of the night."

Elijah's mouth went dry at the harsh reality. "Great." He did nothing to hide his sarcasm.

"That's the ugly truth. You won't get much rest. Being undercover means living the life and keeping yourself alive simultaneously. You become über-cautious."

"Roger that." He nodded. "How'd Graham do with that?"

"None of this has been to his liking."

The image of his bougie brother existing in less-than-stellar accommodations made Elijah grin. "See, that's where I'll have to fake it. I'd rather be outdoors."

Tiandra flicked a glance his way. "Me too."

"Said no woman ever," Elijah teased.

"It's true. South Dakota is a beautiful place. The only bonus of being undercover with the Kings is the mountain setting."

"We're housed daily at this hideout?" Elijah envisioned a squatter's run-down building, falling in on itself.

"They have several dwellings, and they move between them. It's rather ingenious," Tiandra replied. "If the cops raid one location, all of them aren't in the same place at the same time."

"Interesting." Elijah worked to stop his chattering teeth. "Are you stuck there 24/7?"

"No. Everyone comes and goes, which is why our absence the past couple of days isn't a huge issue, but now we should check in and make our appearance." Tiandra turned onto a second highway.

"What else can you tell me?"

"Never talk about the case at the house," Tiandra continued. "We don't communicate there. You and I must maintain our ruse ninety-nine percent of the time. The one percent we leave for updates."

"Is that where you were when Graham sent the extraction message?" Elijah tried grasping everything he needed to learn.

"No, we were at a lodge in Custer State Park. The Kings are arrogant. They're positive this deal will happen, so they celebrated."

"Wow, but none of them has the details?"

"Nope. Mikko's hiding that. However, if anyone knows, it's Penny." Tiandra turned onto a side road, the tires crunching on the snow. "The Kings are used to controlling everything and everyone."

"How do a bunch of hoodlums take over a mountain lodge?"

"The locals don't fight them. It's not worth what they'd pay. Honestly, it's sad."

Elijah tried memorizing their location, but after an hour of driving through rural areas and mountain passes, he was lost.

They traveled a long section of deserted highway before Tiandra pulled off the main road onto a country lane. In the dark, Elijah struggled to see the landscape, which seemed like an endless stretch of evergreens and rocky bluffs. At last, Tiandra drove behind a run-down store that had seen its best years at least a decade prior.

Elijah spotted the two vehicles—an old pickup and a black SUV—and he tensed.

"That's Chance and Riker."

He had to control his external reactions to prevent a Kings gang member from discerning his discomfort. As Tiandra had said, if they sensed weakness, they'd pounce.

She turned off the headlights and parked next to the pickup. "Let's go."

Chance and his German shepherd, Destiny, rounded the rear of the truck and Riker approached from the front end of the SUV. He extended his hand to Elijah, and they shook while Riker's K-9, Ammo, rushed to greet Bosco in a flurry of tail wagging and sniffing.

"You ready for this?" Riker asked.

"Yeah. Just gotta remember to channel my inner Graham and not be me," Elijah replied.

"You'll do great," Tiandra reassured him.

"Eliana is still digging through Graham's cell phone," Riker said.

Elijah tilted his head. "Why not pull everything off the cloud?"

"We don't use traceable phones for our roles," Tiandra explained.

"Anyway," Riker continued, "she found a strange series of numbers but they're incomplete. Possibly a date, partial code—"

"The date of the deal?" Tiandra blurted, cutting him off.

Riker frowned. "Listen before you talk." He playfully punched her arm.

"Sorry, go on." She laughed, shoving him away.

"Anyway, conceivably a date, 0301."

"March 2001?" Elijah asked. "Or a combination?"

"Maybe," Riker said. "There's also a longer number." He held up his hand. "No, I don't have it memorized. Eliana's piecing it together. It appears he either hit the return key to separate them, only had partial information, or it's intentionally incomplete. We'll keep you updated."

"Thank you," Tiandra said.

Chance passed her two large duffels. "If you hate what's inside, blame Skyler."

Tiandra chuckled. "Don't kill the messenger?"

Chance faked a wince. "I bruise like a grape."

That made the group laugh, and Elijah realized how comfortable he was already feeling with the team. They talked easily and took care of each other. He didn't sense an ugly competitiveness. Too bad he wasn't a permanent member.

He shoved away the thought. No. He was only a placeholder.

He'd cover for Graham until his brother returned to work where he belonged.

"Thanks, y'all," Tiandra replied, dropping a hint of her Southern accent. "We'd better get moving."

"Before you go," Riker said. "Eliana put new cell phones in the bag for you and Elijah."

"Good idea." Tiandra passed her old phone and burner to Riker.

"These are clean. For now," Riker added. "But if they're remotely tracking the devices, it won't be long before they invade these too."

"Roger that." Elijah handed Tiandra one and pocketed the other.

"Your contacts are preloaded with Mikko and the gang members," Riker said.

Elijah started for the SUV, halted by Tiandra's shaking head. She pointed at the old truck. He groaned.

Chance glanced at his phone. "Impending weather warning is in effect."

"Great. I'd hate to have one less challenge." Elijah rolled his eyes.

"Stay alive." Riker slapped him on the back. "We're praying for you."

"We'll get the drug deal details and be outta there," Tiandra replied. "That shouldn't take long."

Elijah hoped she was right because being alone with her was getting harder by the minute, and the less time he had to pretend to be Graham, the better.

The splintered plastic of the aged pickup's seat pinched the back of Tiandra's thighs and gasoline fumes permeated the cab interior. "Take the next left," she hollered over the rumbling engine. "We're about an hour from the hideout."

Elijah nodded, eyes fixed on the road ahead.

Heat blasted from the vents, combatting the frigid air seeping through the aged metal doors and gap-inflicted windows.

She glanced in the visor mirror. Thankfully the

cut on her neck was small and her jacket concealed the bandage. Her mind raced with the implications of the latest attack. The team would handle Graham's safety, but Tiandra wondered if the assassin had trailed them from Florida.

If that was the case, why wouldn't the attacker have gone after them there? Had the person followed them to the airport and waited for their return? Or were they spotted between the airport and the diner? With too many unknowns, her brain spun on overdrive with unanswerable questions.

Her thoughts returned to the case and the last moments from the Kings' celebration night. The idea burst and she blurted, "Stop!"

Elijah slammed on the brakes. "What's wrong?" He leaned forward, no doubt searching for danger.

"Sorry, I just had an idea."

He quirked an annoyed brow.

"Hear me out," she said, mentally planning. "Let's head to the lodge."

"Okay." Elijah gestured for her to continue. "Because?" He dragged out the word for two long syllables.

"I keep thinking about the extraction message and how it happened. We'd been at the party for several hours when Graham disappeared on me. We weren't always stuck to one another, but he was gone for a while before I got his message."

"And…"

Tiandra shrugged. "I was run off the road right after he sent the text."

"Are the Kings at the lodge?"

"Penny's texting me to meet her in Deadwood, so everyone must be there," Tiandra reconsidered. "Good point, though. Approach without headlights and if we see anyone, we'll go back another time."

"Okay."

Elijah turned and drove to the lodge with Tiandra's instruction. When they pulled into the parking lot, she gasped, baffled by the decimation. Exterior lights on the two-story picturesque log structure illuminated the party's remenants and needless destruction. Thankfully, the gang hadn't broken out the front lobby's elaborate floor-to-ceiling windows, but they'd trashed the grounds.

Litter fluttered over the snow.

"This is inexcusable."

Elijah parked near the building and shut off the engine. "Where do we begin?"

"Let me think." Tiandra traversed her memories. "Prior to Graham's extraction message, Penny and I were in the main lobby. Let's start there and work upwards."

"Okay."

Tiandra's breath caught at the icy breeze that embraced her as she exited the pickup. She shivered, concluding the ominous environment might've played a larger role than the weather in her physical response. "Gear up. It'll be freezing in there."

"My thoughts exactly." Elijah grinned, already sporting his parka and winter gloves.

She reached for her coat and tugged it on over her leather jacket, long-sleeved T-shirt, and hooded sweatshirt. An image of a child stuffed into a snowsuit came to mind as she struggled to move under the multiple layers.

Tiandra left her gloves in her pocket. Should the need arise for her to shoot, she'd prefer to do so unhindered. She slipped her Glock into the waistband of her jeans.

Bosco whined softly, demanding her attention. Tiandra secured his plain black halter over his chest and attached his leash. Uncertain what they were walking into, she needed to ensure his safety and physical proximity to her.

Her gaze traveled the exterior of the structure where the gang had broken many of the guest room windows. They'd also tossed lounge chairs and tables haphazardly across the lawn and pool area, and a few had pierced the pool's plastic cover.

They traversed the grounds to the kitchen entrance, located at the rear of the lodge. The door hung askew, ripped from the hinges. Tiandra shook her head at the careless wreckage. Elijah moved ahead of her, allowing Tiandra and Bosco to enter first.

Once inside, Elijah withdrew a flashlight, snapping it on and sweeping the beam around the interior. Overturned chairs lay on the linoleum and food splattered the walls and counters. "Wow."

"It's awful, huh?" Tiandra pulled Bosco closer, glancing at the floor. "Watch for broken glass."

Treading carefully through the kitchen and into the main building where the destruction continued, Tiandra reconsidered her decision to return to the lodge. "I don't know what I thought we'd find here. Some big sign that says, 'Here's the assassin hired to kill Graham,' along with the reason?" she said sarcastically.

"We might discover a lead."

She appreciated his supportive reply.

"Must've been a nice place before the Kings got a hold of it," he said.

"The saddest part is the older couple who own it invested their life savings to buy the lodge. They did most of the restoration work themselves." Her throat tightened with sorrow. "It's not right."

Elijah didn't respond, but even in the dim light, Tiandra saw his jaw working. He understood the injustice and wanted the Kings held accountable.

Cans, bottles, and food covered the once-shiny wood floors. Cushions slashed and spewing their stuffing lay near the handcrafted furniture. The colossal staircase on the right side rose to a wide loft that overlooked the common area of the lodge. Strangely, only the elaborate Christmas tree beside the immense stone fireplace that stretched to the thirty-foot vaulted ceiling was unaffected.

"What's up there?"

"Guest rooms are on both sides of the hallway

beyond the lofted area." Tiandra considered the floor plan. "Let's head up."

They'd reached the middle of the stairs when Bosco halted, ears erect.

Tiandra lifted her finger, signaling Elijah. He lowered the flashlight and took off his gloves. Both withdrew their weapons, prepared to fire.

A shuffling sound came from the darkened hallway. Maybe a raccoon or other woodland creature had invaded the lodge? The hairs on the back of Tiandra's neck rose. She motioned for Elijah to move behind her in stack position.

When no other sounds reached them, they advanced along the stairwell to the landing. Tiandra paused and peered around the wall beside the hallway, spotting no movement. With a single wave, she indicated they could continue. They inched forward cautiously, staying to the right side until they reached an open guest room door. A sliver of light cut across the carpeted floor.

Elijah trailed Tiandra and Bosco to where a glow showed from a gap beneath the bathroom door.

They flanked the bathroom, and Tiandra slowly gripped the knob, then swung wide the door.

She entered, arms outstretched, Glock aimed. But the room was empty.

Tiandra lowered her gun, facing Elijah.

A distant click caught their attention, and they hurried out, pausing to glance into the hallway. Tiandra spotted the rear exit stairwell and gestured. Elijah nodded, and they proceeded in that direction.

Tiandra took the lead, reaching for the door and pushing it wide. Bosco entered the stairwell first, and she followed when a shove to her back sent her stumbling forward. The door slammed shut behind her. Tiandra spun and gripped the handle.

Locked!

Scuffling noises erupted from the opposite side. Then a gunshot exploded.

"No!" Tiandra and Bosco bolted down the stairs. She flung open the door to the outside, and they backtracked, entering through the kitchen again.

Gun at the ready, they hurried through the lobby.

Brawling and muffled thuds from above got her attention, and she spotted Elijah fighting with a shadowed figure near the railing.

She hurried to the steps, eyes on Elijah, prepared to fire. "Bosco, stay!"

The two danced a warrior battle, making it impossible for Tiandra to get a clean shot. She raised her Glock and fired above the men, startling both with the blast.

The K-9 barked and lunged forward.

"Bosco, no!" Tiandra cried.

The figure tackled Elijah, forcing him through the wooden railing overhead.

Elijah flailed in midair.

The attacker shot at Tiandra and Bosco, then bolted into the darkness.

FIVE

Elijah flung his arms wide, catching the edge of the landing with one hand. With a grunt, he swung his torso, grasping the ledge with the other hand, and hauled himself up. Tiandra grabbed him by the shoulders and together they worked to get him onto the landing.

Bosco barked, growling low at the darkened hallway. Tiandra restrained him. "Shh."

"Is there more than one here?" Elijah helped Tiandra to her feet.

"I don't know." She glanced over the loft's railing. "I didn't hear an engine, but I think he fled."

Bosco whined, pacing beside her.

"What's going on?"

"He's upset I held him back."

"Let him work," Elijah encouraged.

"Bosco, hunt," she ordered.

The K-9 took off like a shot, leading them down the main stairs. Elijah recovered his gun and flashlight from the lobby floor where both had fallen during the attack. Bosco led them to the kitchen, sniffing a path to a cardboard box on the counter. He sat and barked three times.

"He's alerting!"

Realization slammed into Elijah. "Bomb!"

They bolted out the askew door and rounded

the building just as a thunderous boom rocked the earth. The impact sent Elijah airborne.

He landed face-first on the snow-covered lawn and groaned, twisting to see Tiandra next to him. "Come on." He gripped her arm, and she lifted her head, then scurried to her feet. Bosco sprinted with them, racing to distance themselves from the fiery building. When they'd reached the pool area, they paused, taking in the sight.

A secondary explosion raised the old pickup into the air before slamming it down hard on the parking lot pavement.

"Go!" Tiandra urged, and they ran into the copse of evergreens.

The subsequent boom enveloped the kitchen entrance.

Flames stretched high into the evening sky, emitting a ferocious growling and crackling as they consumed the lodge and surrounding area.

Tiandra gaped, gripping Bosco's leash and tugging him closer.

"Are you okay?" Elijah asked.

"I—"

Gunshots pelted the ground near the tree line.

The trio ducked into the branches and bolted through the brush and forest.

Rapid fire erupted behind them.

Elijah's heart raced as he led them deeper into the wooded area for protection. They didn't stop until they'd gained considerable distance from the lodge. The gunshots echoed but weren't close.

They paused, squatting to hide near a rock formation and catch their breath. Elijah surveyed the winter wonderland, bordered by lavish evergreen trees and craggy cliffs. A white layer of fluffy flakes carpeted the ground, exposing their footsteps and providing a trail for the shooter to follow.

"Stay here." Elijah took off his coat and tugged his hooded sweatshirt over his head, thankful for the multiple layers of clothes he wore. He donned the parka and gloves and using the hooded sweatshirt, he swept the snowy path to cover their tracks.

"Great idea." Tiandra mimicked his moves with her coat. She glanced at Bosco. "Stay." The dog dropped to sit and watched as the team concealed their path.

Elijah and Tiandra made additional prints, separating the trails, leading away from the direction they intended to go. They manuvered quickly, stepping into their same footprints as they backtracked to where Bosco remained, his brown fur now covered in the powdery snow. Neither spoke, choosing to listen for any sign of movement instead.

The atmosphere had quieted, gunshots no longer echoing in the distance.

Still, they were unsure if the shooter followed them.

"That was ingenious," Tiandra commended.

"And it appears we're getting some help too." She held out a hand where snowflakes gathered quickly.

"Wish I'd thought to do it sooner, but hopefully it'll buy some time for us." Elijah shook out his hoodie and pulled it back on. Though it was damp with the snow, the extra layer of clothing was necessary.

Tiandra did the same.

"Do you have any idea where we are?"

"Not a clue and even better, my cell phone has no coverage." She coupled her sarcasm with a visual by holding up the device for him.

"Of course." Elijah sighed.

Bosco gave himself a thorough shake, flinging the snow from his coat in a white cloud.

"Well, we can't just stand out here and become human popsicles." The light from her phone enveloped her in a soft glow. Tiandra tilted her head, snowflakes clinging to her brown hair.

Elijah averted his gaze. "We better take cover. Your team already warned of the impending storm earlier. If the winds don't settle down, it'll be whiteout conditions soon." Going back to what was left of the lodge was certainly out of the question. "Whoever set those explosions intended to eliminate us and any evidence." Tiandra glanced in the distance.

"I don't think he expected us there."

"Agreed. I'm guessing more than one attacker?"

"Especially with the number of bombs that detonated." Elijah leaned down, petting the K-9. "If Bosco hadn't alerted when he did, we'd be dead. You did good, buddy."

The Malinois's tail swished from side to side, making a fan shape in the snow.

Elijah rose and swept the flashlight beam across the landscape. "There's probably a rock formation near here where we can hole up until the storm passes. It'll be safer than the trees."

"Lead on." Tiandra pocketed her cell phone and gathered Bosco's leash.

Together, they trudged the rough terrain toward the rocks. A boscage of a variety of trees paralleled the stones, providing some shelter from the increasingly strong winds and flurries. Elijah spotted a slender passageway between the crags, and they squeezed into the space, tugging their coats tighter.

"It's not inset enough to keep the snow off us," Elijah conceded as the whipping blast pierced their skin like tiny shards of glass.

He led the way out and they stayed close together. The blizzard conditions impeded their vision. Elijah's nostrils and cheeks burned from the frigid air.

After walking for what seemed like hours, he glanced down at Bosco, who was covered in snow, and feared for the dog. They had to find shelter, fast. They'd left their bags in the pickup, so they were literally stuck with only the clothes on their backs.

Lord, help us locate a place to hide from the storm.

At last, Elijah spotted a break in the precipice wall ahead. He motioned to it, and Tiandra nodded. Together they made their way through the treacherous elements, following a fissure in the cracked stone to a narrow opening between two boulders. They scurried into the space and ventured deeper into the small cave and settled at the farthest point.

They huddled close and Tiandra unzipped her outer coat, enveloping Bosco against her chest. Elijah knelt in front of them, encircling the team and creating a cocoon for Bosco to maximize body heat. When the dog had had enough of the group hug, he shifted.

"He's done," Tiandra joked through chattering teeth.

Elijah lowered his arms, allowing Bosco to escape and give himself a thorough shake. "I was worried about him out there."

"Me too." Tiandra removed her hoodie and tied it around the Malinois.

"We have nothing to build a fire." Elijah sat on the cold stone. "Our best alternative is to hole up until the storm passes."

In response, an eerie howl traveled into the cave's opening, along with some snow.

Elijah rose. "Stay here while I cover that."

"I'll go with you."

"No. Please let me impress you with my outdoorsman skills."

Tiandra grinned as Elijah crawled out, withdrawing his Leatherman knife from the pocket of his jeans.

Thick evergreens spanned the landscape. He moved through the icy wind to the closest tree and cut off several branches, repeating the maneuver until he'd collected a decent stash.

The storm had grown increasingly worse, and he prayed it would end soon. However, the blizzard also provided protection since the killer probably wouldn't venture to chase them, assuming they'd perish in the elements. Elijah had done his best to ensure they stayed near the rock, creating a path they'd retrace down the mountain when it passed.

The flashlight beam worsened his vision. Just a few more branches. Elijah inched along the rocky wall, grounding himself so as not to lose track of his location. The blinding flakes fell in a heavy white curtain, hindering his ability to see.

Keeping to the rocks, he crept toward the next tree, gripped a branch and cut through the wood. This time, though, his knife slipped, piercing through his glove. With a yelp, he jerked back his hand, dropping the flashlight and underestimating his footing. His boot skidded on the icy rock, and he slammed on his backside, then slid down the ravine. His head smacked an impacted boulder, exploding pain behind his eyes.

Elijah caught himself before he dropped to the next ledge. The flashlight landed near his right arm, and he stretched to grasp the barrel.

Chest heaving with exertion, he gripped a tree root, using his boots to find purchase. Slowly, Elijah turned onto his stomach, scrambling for wedged stones to support his weight. He attempted crawling up the ravine, but his right ankle throbbed. He prayed it was only sprained. Balancing unevenly on his left boot, he clung to roots, boulders, and low-hanging branches until he reached the ledge and crawled to solid ground.

With a grunt, Elijah grabbed the boughs he'd cut and tucked them under one arm, then, using his free hand to balance, hobbled toward the cave.

A light bounced ahead, and Tiandra rushed to him. "What happened?"

"Long story. Can you take these?" He passed her the branches.

"You're hurt."

"Little bit," he grumbled.

She braced his weight and helped him amble the remaining distance. Once inside, they secured the brush against the cave entrance, which helped shield them from the elements, but also eliminated any ambient light. They moved farther into the inky space and huddled with Bosco.

Elijah's ankle, head, and hand ached. "I need to get my boot off."

"No." Tiandra shifted the flashlight. "Let me look first."

"Guess I overestimated my great outdoorsman abilities." He half joked, embarrassed by his rookie mistake.

"It's horrific out there. You did an amazing job protecting us in here." Tiandra knelt in front of him, her hands gentle but strong against his ankle. "There's a lot of heat coming off that. Hopefully, it's only a sprain, but your boot will reduce the swelling."

"Are you secretly a doctor?" Elijah asked, impressed by her skills.

"We all have secrets."

Tiandra knelt before Elijah and gently examined his face for injuries, acutely aware of their proximity. His breath was warm on her cheeks, his gray-blue eyes tender as he traced her movements. Tiandra swallowed hard, focusing on his medical needs to avoid the warmth radiating through her chest. "Um, you have a laceration on your right eyebrow, and a knot on the back of your head, though it appears to be more bark than bite," she teased, patting the wound with her fingertips.

He winced. "Let me tear my T-shirt for bandages."

"Good idea." She leaned on her heels, appreciating the space.

Elijah pulled off his winter parka, then the

hoodie, revealing the long-sleeved T-shirt underneath.

Tiandra turned away, tending to Bosco, whose fur had dried. "Doing all right, buddy?"

He gave a happy tail-thump in reply.

"Okay," Elijah said.

Tiandra twisted to face him and took the T-shirt he held out to her, brushing her fingers against his hand. The touch was warm, even in the frigid atmosphere. Why was she acting like this?

She ripped bandages from the fabric, channeling her unfamiliar emotions into the task. Using caked snow on the edges of his parka, she dampened the cloth and wiped at the dried blood, then pressed it tightly against the wound. "Maintain pressure on that while I work on your hand." Tiandra examined the cut. "You really need stitches, but we'll have to make do until we get out of here." She wrapped his hand with a strip of the T-shirt fabric.

"You're good at this," Elijah said. "Part of those secrets you mentioned?"

"Yeah." Tiandra bit her lip. Why had she said that? The cold must've frozen her intelligence. "No biggie. I was a nurse a hundred years ago."

He laughed. "Please elaborate."

"I started out in nursing right after college. Thought for sure medicine was my calling in life."

"What changed?"

Tiandra finished the bandage and shifted to sit on her heels. "It's a long story."

"The weather doesn't appear to be slowing any, so I'd say we have time." Elijah tilted his head, still pressing the fabric against the injury with his good hand.

"I'm sorry you got hurt out there."

He shrugged. "Chicks dig scars, right?"

Tiandra laughed, the reaction energizing her. Elijah made her feel alive. "For sure."

His fun temperament and knowledge in providing shelter for them in the storm ignited a strange emotion. She felt cared for. Protected. And she liked it.

Too much.

"Please don't take this the wrong way, but we need to keep warm."

Tiandra sucked in a breath.

"Mind if I sit beside you and Bosco?"

She exhaled. *Get your head in the game, Daugherty.* Elijah was only a coworker on a mission. "Um, sure. Since he's got short fur, let's put him between us and warm him too." She scooted to Bosco's right. *And it keeps me from making a fool of myself.*

Elijah moved to the dog's left.

The position change helped, and Tiandra tried to get comfortable on the stony floor. Talking about her past might alleviate the romantic notions invading her normally business-first brain. "I'll start at the beginning. My dad was a cop." She leaned against the cave's icy wall. "My hero from birth."

Images of the larger-than-life man whom she'd adored filled her mind. "He worked long hours, but somehow he was always there for us."

"That couldn't have been easy with eleven kids," Elijah commented.

"Right? I only have Bosco to care for. I don't know how he balanced it all." Tiandra chuckled, stroking the Malinois's soft fur for comfort and courage. "He was off duty the night the domestic dispute call came in. The younger responding officer requested backup, and we lived close to the house. So, Dad went to help."

"They allowed him to do that?"

"Did I forget to mention he was the chief of police?" Tiandra grinned.

"That changes everything."

"He wasn't supposed to be there." Grateful for the darkness, Tiandra inhaled deeply for the fortitude to tell the rest of the story. "The call took a turn for the worst." Her throat thickened with sorrow as it always did when she thought of her father. "The male offender shot him."

"I'm sorry." Elijah's tender voice, accompanied by his hand on her shoulder, nearly undid her. "I'm a jerk. I never should've—"

"You didn't know," she interrupted him. "I was working the night shift in the ER." Her eyes stung with fresh tears, as though witnessing it again. "I got to tell him I loved him before—" Her throat tightened, cutting off her words.

"I can't imagine."

After several seconds of wiping away the moisture and regaining composure, she said, "That was a pivotal point for me. Justice overtook my desire to help people heal. I applied to the FBI academy. I was older than many of the recruits, but I'm stubborn and competitive." She swiped at her cheeks. "About five years afterward, Beckham Walsh recruited me for HFTF."

"You're truly amazing."

"Hardly. Just headstrong."

His hand covered hers on Bosco's side, and he squeezed gently. "I'm sorry for my insensitivity in pushing you to talk to me."

Tiandra glanced down. "It's good for me to remember why I do what I do. Especially when I'm hunkered inside a cave waiting for a blizzard to stop."

Elijah laughed. "Fair enough."

She leaned her head against the stone wall. "So…"

"Sew buttons on your shirt," he teased.

"Very funny. Now it's your turn. Tell me your story."

Elijah withdrew his hand from hers, and she instantly regretted asking him to talk.

"Not much to share. I always wanted to be a cop, and I fell in love with Sioux City, Iowa. Small-town with all the amenities."

"Never been there," she confessed.

"It's a nice place. I love the people I work with."

Was someone special waiting for Elijah? Why hadn't she considered that possibility? "Both you and Graham dreamed of becoming cops?"

"Graham didn't pursue law enforcement until after I got on with Sioux City PD." Elijah snorted. "He always goes above and beyond."

Did she sense a bitterness in his tone? "How so?"

Elijah shifted, fidgeting with his boot. "Do you remember the old song lyrics, 'anything you can do I can do better'?"

Tiandra chuckled. "Yeah, my sisters tormented me with it."

"Let's just say that applies to Graham. He's a golden child."

"And you're not?"

Why was she pushing him? Because Elijah intrigued her.

"I'll see if the storm's lessening any." He crawled past her in the confining space, ending the discussion.

Tiandra closed her eyes, allowing her thoughts to flutter around her father, enjoying the memories. If only she had one more day with him...

"Tiandra."

She jerked and blinked, unable to clear the darkness from her eyes. How long had she been asleep? Fear took hold in the unfamiliar surroundings. "Where are we?"

"We're still in the cave. The storm passed. We might want to get out of here and find cell service."

"Yes." Tiandra put her hands on the frigid floor and pushed herself upright. Her muscles were stiff from the cold and extensive exercise, but she wouldn't complain.

Elijah flicked on the flashlight, crouched near the entrance with Bosco. He'd pulled down a section of the evergreen covering, and moonlight poured inside. She joined them and they stepped outside. The frosty air, minus the wind, was bearable.

"Let's retrace our steps," Elijah said. "Stick close to the rocky wall."

"Got it."

They walked through the night, their boots crunching on the snowy ground. She trailed behind Elijah, realizing she trusted him to lead. Though they barely knew each other, his confidence reassured her. He hobbled a bit, but based on his gait, his ankle felt better, proving it was a mild sprain.

They trudged through the snow for what seemed like hours before reaching the clearing to the lodge.

"Kudos. You're the great outdoorsman," Tiandra commended.

"Thanks."

They exited the forest and approached the smoldering lodge and old pickup. Tiandra reached for her cell. Barely one bar of battery remained, and she'd missed two text messages from Penny.

Hey girl, where ya been?

Then a second,

Call me.

She couldn't waste battery responding to Penny. Tiandra quickly typed a text to the team's burner phone, providing the code for the lodge, and requested help.

Seconds later, her cell rang and she answered.

"Are you okay?" Walsh asked.

"Yes. Phone's almost dead."

"Got it. Be there ASA—"

Tiandra glanced at the device. The last of the battery was gone. "They'll be here soon," she assured Elijah. "Or they'll send help."

"It's safe to say we have nothing left in there." He gestured to the fire-stained pickup.

They watched the road for any sign of the attacker or help, spotting neither.

"Hopefully he thinks we're dead." Tiandra sighed.

Headlights approached in the distance as if in response to her words.

"Take cover until we know who it is," she said.

They hurried into the shadows, watching as the approaching vehicle pulled into the parking lot. The familiar SUV brought a huge measure of relief to Tiandra. "We're safe."

They hustled out and climbed into the backseat, Bosco joining them.

Skyler and Chance sat in the front seats. "Let's get you guys clean and warmed up."

"Yes, please."

Sirens bellowed in the distance.

"They're a little late," Elijah replied.

"Yeah, but they'll provide the cover for us to get away." Tiandra glanced at the lodge. "At least there was no one else here. Clearly, we interrupted someone's plans tonight."

SIX

Elijah studied his reflection in the truck's visor mirror. Tiandra had done a great job of creating bruises with makeup. "Are you certain these tattoos will stay on?" He fingered the dragon tail image that swept from his T-shirt neckline up toward his ear. "They look too real to be stickers."

"That's the idea." Tiandra smoothed her shirt-sleeve, concealing her own rub-on tattoos. "Once they adhere, they'll stick for a week. However, if you notice any pieces coming off, let me know right away."

"I won't even try replacing it by myself."

"You could, but the key is getting them in the same spot," Tiandra remarked. "That's why the selfie photos on our phones are necessary."

Elijah glanced at the cell screen with the picture of him and Tiandra posing for the camera. "You think of everything."

"I'd like to stay alive to finish this."

"Doesn't Bosco get a disguise too?" Elijah stroked the Belgian Malinois's chin as he hovered over the car console between them.

"He has that outrageous collar." Tiandra gave the dog a quick kiss on the muzzle.

Bosco sported a wide black leather collar with spikes protruding outward.

"I dunno, I think he wants a rub-on tattoo," Elijah joked.

The K-9 whined, eliciting laughter.

"How's the ankle and hand healing?"

"Two days was more than enough time. I'm good to go." He lifted his hand where a small bandage covered the stitches.

"All right then. If you're ready, I'll call Penny and initiate the entrance discussion for our ruse."

"I'm all in." Elijah stretched back in the driver's seat. "Wait. First, how does Graham behave around Penny?" Surely his flirty brother wouldn't dare act that way with a drug lord's girlfriend.

"He doesn't talk to her unless it's necessary. In fact, the less you speak, the better. Don't worry, though, your voice is identical to his. It's a matter of using the same speech patterns."

"Go me," Elijah replied sarcastically.

"None of that. Graham doesn't joke around," Tiandra admonished. "He basically responds to Mikko and the other members in short responses. Yes, no, et cetera. Graham struggled with that part, believe it or not."

"Yeah, picturing my chatty-patty brother trying to stay quiet is a stretch." Graham loved being the center of attention. "But for me it's good news. I don't have to talk." Elijah waggled his eyebrows. "This just keeps getting better."

"You're G and I'm Tia."

"G. That's it?" Elijah chuckled.

"Short for Gray. We try to stick close to our real names."

"I hope I remember to respond if someone calls me that."

"I'll help remind you, but seriously work on it, because that'll be a dead giveaway."

The prompt sobered Elijah to the situation. "What about Bosco?"

"His name remains the same."

The dog whined again.

"I'd say he disagrees," Elijah teased.

Tiandra scratched Bosco's scruff. "You're definitely smart enough, handsome, but let's stick with what we've got."

If Elijah wasn't mistaken, the canine harrumphed before retreating to the backseat and curling up to nap.

Tiandra lifted her cell phone. "Ready?"

"As I'll ever be," Elijah replied.

She put the call on speakerphone, allowing Elijah to eavesdrop on the conversation with Penny. The line rang twice before a squeaky voice answered, "Finally!"

"G and I were nearly killed!" Tiandra said.

She had Elijah's full attention. Her normal sweet tone with a slight Southern twang had changed, taking on a harder, deeper edge as she slid into her undercover persona.

An audible gasp. "No way! What happened?"

"Haven't you heard?" Tiandra met Elijah's gaze.

Penny's response would tell them everything. "Heard what? Are you okay? Did you get into something bad?"

Elijah recognized the reference to drugs. Was Penny clueless of the attack?

"Nah, someone forced us off the road. Destroyed my truck and G's bike. We barely made it out alive." Irritation hung in Tiandra's tone.

"What? That's messed up! I saw you leave the party early, but when you didn't answer my texts, I figured you were visiting family, doing holiday junk."

Tiandra snorted. "Not even close. Plus, I don't hang with family."

"Me either. Too much baggage."

"For real."

"Are you hurt?"

"Nah, G rattled his brain a little bit, but there wasn't much to start with."

The women burst into giggles, and Elijah tightened his jaw. Tiandra winked at him, and his neck warmed.

"Man, I'm so glad to hear that. You should've called me. I would've hung out with you. Read you magazines or something," Penny replied.

"Deliver me a casserole?" Tiandra laughed.

"Yep, like my granmama." Penny quieted, then said, "Was it an accident?"

"No way. Remember, Bosco and I left the party?

I had the worst stomachache, whew!" Tiandra's emphatic response continued to impress Elijah.

"I forgot about that. Probably Enrique's pasta. He's gotta have a cement stomach to eat that food."

Tiandra chuckled. "No doubt."

"How'd G get involved?"

"I didn't even know they'd taken him out on his bike until I got to the hospital."

"That proves someone's got it out for you!" Penny said. "But who?"

"That's the question," Tiandra replied. "I have no haters. Can't speak for G."

"Uh-huh. That's probably it. We're always in the line of fire for our men," Penny said.

"Right?" Tiandra replied.

Elijah grinned at her. She played the part well.

"Mikko's been asking about G."

Elijah and Tiandra shared a look. Was Mikko unaware of the accident or fishing for information?

"I'll tell him," Tiandra said. "We're on our way back to the house now."

"I'll tell Mikko what happened too," Penny replied.

"Maybe he'll know who's out to get us." Tiandra referenced the hit. "They forced us off the road. It wasn't an accident. That's for sure."

Penny tsked into the line. "Mikko won't like hearing someone tried hurting one of his own."

"Two," Tiandra corrected.

"Yeah," Penny said.

"Unless it's an outsider," Tiandra dropped the hint, and Elijah waited... Would she take the bait?

"No!" Penny exclaimed. "You think it's a Twenty-Niner closin' in?" Her tone assumed a conspiratorial whisper.

"I didn't think of that!" Tiandra rolled her eyes. "Why us, though?"

Elijah gave her a thumbs-up and suppressed a grin.

"I'll try to find out."

"Thanks. See you in a few."

"Be careful, Tia," Penny added. "If Locos are after you..."

"I'm watchin'." Tiandra disconnected.

"Doesn't sound like Mikko's behind the attack," Elijah said as he started the engine.

"Nope. Penny's no actress. She sounded genuinely worried."

"However, you were Oscar-worthy brilliant. Did you act in high school plays or something?"

Tiandra gave a playful, awkward curtsy in her seat. "Thank you, kind sir."

"You really are good at this." Realizing he gushed too emphatically, he redirected. "When she said Twenty-Niner I assume she meant someone in the 29 Locos Cartel." Elijah pulled out of the parking space and headed for the highway.

"Yes. A rival gang member means our cover isn't compromised with the Kings. That's great news."

"Now we need to figure out why the cartel is

after Graham. What did he discover that put him and you in the line of fire?" Elijah focused on the winding rural road, determined to learn the route and landscape as much as possible. Survival meant knowing his surroundings.

"Drive another mile, then take a left." Her cell phone rang, and she glanced down. "Hold up. Penny's calling back."

Elijah slowed as she answered on speakerphone. "Hey, Penny."

"Mikko says come straight to his place. He's so mad! I told him 'bout you and G."

"Okay, we'll head that way."

They disconnected.

"That solves the problem of talking to Mikko," Elijah said.

"No, it just gets us in the door."

She provided directions to Mikko's house and Elijah pulled up to the two-story clapboard outside Deadwood.

"There's no turning back once we go in there."

"Was that an option?" Elijah's pulse ramped up. "Showtime."

They exited the car with Bosco and strolled up the walkway. Several gang members lingered around the patio area, smoking cigarettes.

"G! Glad you finally showed up." One of the men grabbed Elijah's hand and started a complicated handshake. Elijah fumbled on a couple of the moves and the guy quirked a brow.

"His melon got rattled."

Elijah spun, instantly recognizing Mikko Stefanov as he stepped out the front door. "Probably barely remembers who he is, much less how to shake."

The others chortled, and Elijah appreciated the interruption.

Mikko put an arm on his shoulders. "Dude, Penny told me what happened. Get in here and let's talk about retribution."

"Yeah," Elijah grunted, earning him an approving nod from Tiandra.

They entered the house.

Straight into the lion's den.

Tiandra watched, her heart drumming hard as Elijah and Mikko conversed on the other side of the room. Penny rambled at high speed about nonsense, ensuring Tiandra didn't have a prayer of overhearing the men's discussion. But Mikko smiled a lot, and Elijah's deep baritone voice carried with his limited responses.

"So then get this. Lisa's talking 'bout Mikko eyein' her. Claims he's interested, and I better watch out." Penny harrumphed. "She's the one who better 'watch out' if I catch her looking at my man," she continued with steady enthusiasm, though Tiandra had already lost interest in the gossip. "He's faithful. Like my granmama used to say, 'love protects.'"

"Yes, it does." Tiandra smiled, shifting into Tia Mode. "You need help with Lisa?"

"Nope." Penny grinned wide, slapping the table.

Constant childish fighting among the gang women wore on Tiandra, considering none of the men deserved the admiration given to them. Yet, Tiandra played her role.

Penny placed a hand on her arm. "Tia, for real. Is G trustworthy? Could he have a girlfriend who tried running y'all off the road?"

Tiandra considered her response. If only that were the issue. Though if Graham was compromised, technically, Penny was correct. "Huh, if he did, she didn't care enough about him to visit him at the hospital," she answered. "But you tell me if you see anything suspicious."

Penny gave her a fist bump. "We girls gotta stick together. Like blood sisters."

"Exactly."

"Truthfully, though, I wish I'd had a sister like you." The wistfulness in Penny's voice prickled Tiandra's heart. She liked the woman, and they'd had several discussions about losing their siblings.

"Really?" Tiandra watched Penny's expression.

"Yeah. I was a messed-up kid after losing my brother. Hank was my hero. No one could touch him." Penny ran her hand through her long, blond hair. "He protected me. It was just the two of us."

Tiandra glanced down. "I get that. I miss my baby sister every day." Tiandra had told Penny about Anissa, though she'd never shared the truth of her sister's drug overdose or the fact that she had nine other living siblings.

"Guess we have to do what my granmama used to say," Penny said.

"Oh, yeah, what's that?"

"Hold on to memories, so they're close to our hearts. That's what keeps them alive," Penny said. "Then tell others all we remember."

"She sounds like a smart lady."

"Best there ever was." Past tense.

In her peripheral vision, Tiandra spotted Elijah and Mikko rising to their feet with a handshake. Grateful to divert from the painful conversation, she brought up Lisa again. "You're sure you don't want me to talk to Lisa?"

Penny giggled. "Nah, don't steal my fun."

Elijah approached, and Tiandra tried to appear nonchalant as Penny continued rambling about the sneaky women in the group.

"Ready?" He put a hand on her shoulder.

Tiandra could've jumped into his arms with gratitude. "Okay. See you tomorrow?"

"I'll be here." Penny tilted her head and stood. "Take care of her." She slapped his shoulder.

Elijah did a double take, and Tiandra offered him a crooked smile. He glanced at Penny as though she'd spoken in a foreign language, then looked at his shoulder. "Uh-huh."

Tiandra gave her an apologetic grin and gathered Bosco's leash. "Come on, boy."

They headed out into the cold winter night, saying half-hearted goodbyes to the guys on the porch.

Once inside the car and on the road, Elijah said, "That was more workout for my heart than a ten-mile run."

"Tell me everything." Tiandra twisted to face him.

"Where am I going now?"

"I guess back to the hideout."

"Mikko doesn't stay there?"

"No, and I promise you won't get much rest tonight. You have to always remain guarded."

"Fabulous."

"We'll meet first thing in the morning. The others sleep until the afternoon, but we don't want to be caught talking around them."

"Okay."

Tiandra provided directions for Elijah, then said, "Spill."

"Mikko was very interested in the accident and unless he's a great actor, he appeared totally surprised by it all."

"Did he mention the drug deal?"

"Not by name, but he said rumor in the cartel is someone is down for a big buy. Apparently, it's unsubstantiated the Kings are taking the load. They're worried the cartel will start a full-on war to get the drugs."

"They'd be correct." Tiandra's cell phone rang. "Weird, it's Penny." She placed the call on speaker. "Did I forget my dog?" she joked.

"If you had, I'd never tell. Bosco's a doll. Reminds me of my brother's mutt, Max." Penny laughed. "I'd keep him in a heartbeat."

Bosco whined from the backseat, in disagreement with that option.

Tiandra chuckled.

"Something big came up," Penny continued. "Mikko says he wants to meet you guys at the hideout in a while. After the losers here pass out."

"Okay."

They disconnected. "That's new," Tiandra said. "He didn't mention that to me."

"He didn't want the others to overhear?"

"Possibly." Elijah rounded the curve. "Catch me up on everything prior to Graham texting you to leave the party."

Concerns for Graham's health invaded Tiandra's thoughts. She forced herself into FBI agent mode. "I sat against the wall, Penny was near me in a verbal spat with Lisa, a woman who Penny's convinced is hitting on Mikko. Anyway, on the far side of the lodge, a fight broke out between four or five of the Kings. Another random argument with the idiots." She rolled her eyes.

"Put enough foreign substances in already brain-compromised individuals and it's inevitable," Elijah agreed.

"Exactly. I hoped someone would slip and give me the location of the meeting." Tiandra leaned back in the seat and crossed her ankles. "Inebriated Kings talk. All I had to do was wait it out. Sadly, that didn't happen."

"Or the lesser-level Kings have no clue. Mikko's holding that information close to the vest, so to speak," Elijah said. "Hey, if that's true, maybe Mikko wants to meet with us to pull us into the inner circle?"

"Let's hope so. That'll change everything."

"You're at the party, a fight breaks out, and then what?" Elijah asked.

"I got Graham's extraction message and made an excuse about a stomachache, then used the fight as a diversion to leave the lodge."

"Did Graham initiate the brawl, so you'd escape unnoticed?"

"I never considered that." *Mostly because I've been so busy blaming and accusing Graham that it never occurred to me he was helping me.* The condemning thought was like a mental slap upside her head. "That's plausible." Tiandra shrugged. "Toward the end, we didn't see each other much."

"Is that uncommon?"

"Yes, but to maximize our undercover efforts, it was best for us to divide and conquer whenever possible," Tiandra explained.

"Should I expect the same?"

"Definitely."

"So then we connect somewhere out of sight of the Kings and compare notes, share intel?"

"Yes, although Graham wasn't forthcoming toward the end." If Elijah noticed the bitterness in her tone, he didn't show it. The fresh reminder of her partner's strange behavior sent irritation through Tiandra. "Information is power in Ops."

"Makes sense." Elijah grew quiet for several beats, then asked, "Why'd Graham withhold intel?"

She wanted to tell Elijah that Graham's elusiveness became more evident over the past couple of months. She'd not yet confessed her concerns that Graham might be working for the other side. Unloading that on Elijah was unfair. But something wasn't right.

"He had cause to break protocol," Elijah said without hesitation.

"Definitely." Though what that reason was eluded her. It could've compromised the case, her life, and his. Tiandra bit her lip, not wanting to go there. "The only thing Graham mentioned prior to that night was the possibility of an insider. We haven't figured out why he thought that, and there's no evidence to support it."

"How much pull does Penny have with Mikko?"

"A lot. They're known as a couple in the gang. That's a big deal, especially for the leader." Tiandra considered the discussion. "I've had success in getting her to confide in me. She's the link we need."

Elijah nodded, prompting her to continue.

"That's pretty much it. Bosco and I bolted."

"Graham's message didn't provide details? Is that normal?"

"All it said was 'get out.' We don't give those instructions lightly."

"Whoever wanted you two dead followed you from the party," Elijah surmised.

"That's my guess," Tiandra said.

"Then it could've been a King member who forced you and Graham off the road."

"If a single King made us or even suspected our true identities, they'd have shot us at Mikko's tonight."

"Hmm, can't argue. In fact, they'd call you out in front of everyone rather than dispose of you out of sight," Elijah conceded.

They tossed ideas back and forth until they reached the hideout. The older two-story house sat at the end of a deserted main street with brick-faced businesses along one side of the neglected property. Thanks to the viciousness of the Kings, the businesses had closed, leaving it a modern-day ghost town.

"Park here," she instructed, and Elijah pulled up to the run-down, detached two-car garage on the left of the house. Large overgrown evergreens provided the seclusion that Mikko and the Kings relished.

"Doesn't look like anyone else is here. It's hard

to tell in the dark, but the place was probably decent once," Elijah commented.

"That's the result of everything the Kings touch. They're a wave of destruction."

He shut off the engine. "Now what?"

"We wait inside for Mikko," Tiandra said. "Not a huge surprise the others aren't here. Mikko's like their flame, and they're all moths fluttering around him."

"That was almost poetic," Elijah teased.

"Thanks," she chuckled.

They exited the vehicle and Tiandra released Bosco, keeping him leashed. Many of the Kings had dogs and not all were friendly. Bosco could easily hold his own, but she'd not willingly put him in danger.

They paused near the falling chain-link fence, and Elijah reached for the gate latch. With an appropriate screech, the gate opened, and they entered the property, making their way up the sidewalk. She glanced at the house with its chipped paint and broken shutters. A cracked bedroom window upstairs revealed askew curtains peeking from the frame's edge. Debris appeared through the snow-covered ground, littering the yard from the Kings' many parties. No lights glowed from inside.

She led the way to the front door and reached for the handle. Locked.

"Do they normally leave it locked?" Elijah whispered.

"Sometimes, but the back door might be open." Frosty wind whipped against them as if urging them inside, stinging Tiandra's cheeks. "They're usually not worried about someone breaking in. This is just a hangout place. Nothing of value is here."

They walked to the east side of the house, but snowdrifts impeded their approach. Turning around, they headed west, where the snow was less severe. A soft glow from the back patio stretched across the lawn, encouraging shadows that embraced them from the overgrown evergreens that hugged the exterior. Elijah led the way, Tiandra and Bosco trailing.

The hairs on the back of Tiandra's neck rose in a silent visceral warning. Bosco emitted a low growl, the rising scruff of his neck visible even in the dim light. They paused, listening. Bosco's ears rotated like furry radars collecting information.

She glanced beyond Elijah, unable to see anything past the evergreens. Then she slowly pivoted to look behind her.

A whizzing over her shoulder sent Bosco lunging forward, yanking Tiandra. She collided with Elijah, and they stumbled against the house, trying to regain their balance.

"Hey—" Elijah's sentence disintegrated as the second crossbow arrow whizzed within centimeters of his head.

SEVEN

Elijah tugged Tiandra down as she simultaneously tackled Bosco. Tangled in the evergreens' prickly branches, they scrambled to escape through the maze of foliage.

"Go!" Elijah hollered, low crawling on the icy ground.

Tiandra and Bosco hurried behind him, and they made their way around the trees toward the back of the house.

Additional arrows flew at them, whizzing in an eerie whistle, confirming the shooter used a crossbow.

Judging from the trajectory of the arrows, the hidden marksman had an elevated advantage, leaving them exposed. They quickly rounded the house, opposite the garage where Elijah had parked, and ran, targeting the back door for shelter.

Tiandra slipped on the ice. Elijah caught her before she fell, and they stumbled to the door.

She gripped the handle. "Locked!"

Unprotected on the cement patio empty of furniture to hide behind, they searched for another way of escape. But there was nothing solid to conceal them.

"We can't go to the car," Tiandra said. "We'd be sitting ducks there."

Elijah held her hand. "Let's head for that brick building." He gestured with his chin at the shop across the yard from where they stood. They sprinted toward the building.

Tires on the road in front of the house screeched.

They entered the alley when headlights appeared, heading straight for them. The engine roared as the driver accelerated, drawing near and trapping them in the narrow space with nowhere to hide.

They slid to a halt, scanning the area for a getaway. Tiandra drew Bosco closer and ordered, "Behind." He obediently shifted to the position. Tiandra withdrew her Glock from her waistband. Elijah did the same. They stood back-to-back, her watching the front of the house, him watching the alley.

The car stopped four feet from them, and the passenger door opened. Penny emerged, waving wildly. "Get in!"

Tiandra shot Elijah a look. "It's Mikko."

"A trap?"

Tiandra glanced over her shoulder. The sound of men's voices approached from the front of the house. "What other choice do we have?"

"Hurry!" Penny urged.

Mikko revved the engine in response.

Elijah let out a growl of frustration, then they bolted for Mikko's car.

Penny jumped into the passenger seat and

slammed the door just as Tiandra, Bosco, and Elijah dived into the backseat, barely closing the door before Mikko took off. Gunshots pelted the windshield.

Mikko cursed, then reversed, speeding backward to the road. He swung into a J-turn with such precision it would've impressed Elijah's police academy instructors.

"Nice," Elijah commended.

"Comes from dodging cops," Mikko laughed. "Stole my first car when I was thirteen."

The man said it with such pride, Elijah had to force himself not to respond. They sped from the house, squealing tires around the corner. Mikko fishtailed on the ice, but he recovered well.

Headlights approached from behind, and gunshots pelted the car, pinging off the back window. Elijah and Tiandra ducked down, holding Bosco low.

"What's going on?" Mikko barked.

"Wish I knew. Someone shot at us with a crossbow." Remembering Tiandra's instruction to speak less, Elijah clamped shut his mouth, waiting for Mikko to respond.

"Penny and I saw dudes out front of the hideout." Mikko sped up and merged onto the main highway. After a few moments, it appeared they lost the pursuers.

Tiandra and Elijah slid up in the seat again.

"You made someone's kill list according to my

boys," Mikko said, referring to the Kings. "Word on the street is there's a paid hit for you, G."

Reminded of this undercover role name, Elijah said, "Some coward who won't face me like a man."

Mikko guffawed. "You've got more than one enemy, bro. We're talking 29 Locos. If one is after you, they all are."

"You sure it's them?" Tiandra asked.

"There's no secrets in the Kings." Mikko glanced in the rearview mirror and Elijah held his breath. What had Mikko discovered?

"Rumor is there's a gang war brewing," Mikko said. "It's got my crew all worked up."

Elijah and Tiandra didn't dare look at one another. They could do nothing but wait for Mikko to reveal more information.

"Tell them, baby," Penny urged.

"Shh, woman!" Mikko admonished. "You talk too much."

"What's she mean?" Elijah asked.

"Two Kings were killed in a drive-by shooting last night." Mikko slammed his hands on the steering wheel. "Locos are out for blood."

"You're certain it was them?" Tiandra asked.

Mikko glanced in the rearview mirror again. "Yeah, I am. That's why I'm the boss."

"Tia, know your place." Elijah hoped she didn't clock him upside the head for the comment intended to regain Mikko's respect.

"Sorry, Mikko," Tiandra said, her voice soft.

"Who'd they kill?" Elijah asked.

"Vito and Orlando," Mikko said, naming the two men Elijah recognized as Mikko's henchmen based on the crime file information.

Tiandra's raised eyebrows and open mouth conveyed that she understood the implications of the murders too.

"Locos are trying to take out the key players?" Elijah asked.

"They want to get their hands on the drugs and decimate the Kings," Mikko responded.

"So why put a hit out on me?" Elijah asked.

"No one's talking about that," Mikko replied. "You got enemies, bro."

"Could be something to rock the deal," Penny offered.

"Yeah, it's rattled my guys," Mikko remarked. "Wondering if the 29 Locos are trying to steal my drugs. I need people I can trust." He pulled the car over. "Can't have no backstabbers."

Elijah glanced out the window. They were somewhere in the mountains, though he was clueless where. The headlights illuminated a deep ravine ahead. Had Mikko brought them here to kill them?

Mikko shifted into Park, then reached for the console.

Elijah's hand instinctively moved for his own Glock tucked into his waistband. Tiandra tensed beside him. No doubt she was itching to draw her weapon.

Mikko withdrew a Sig Sauer pistol, waving it to coincide with his order. "Step outside and talk."

Penny turned on the overhead light, then leaned forward, lifting her purse and removing a lipstick tube. She swiped her lips generously and smacked them to seal the application. Did women put on makeup before their boyfriend shot someone? Elijah tried not to swallow hard, using every instinct to discern Mikko's intentions.

"It's freezing out there," Tiandra whined. "Can't we stay in here with the heater?"

"C'mon, Tia, it ain't bad," Penny urged.

Tiandra and Elijah shared a look. "Bosco has short fur. He can't be outside when it's cold," she argued.

"Good point. Leave him in the car. We gotta talk face-to-face. Right, G?" Mikko pierced Elijah with a dark stare.

Had Graham established a secret code? *Lord, grant me wisdom here.* A wrong answer could compromise his cover. "You're the boss," Elijah said with a shrug.

"Move." Mikko sat with one foot out of the car.

"C'mon, Tia, it's all good," Elijah encouraged, praying he wasn't leading them to their deaths.

"Fine," Tiandra grunted, "but I'm taking Bosco."

"Whatever you want," Elijah added for Mikko's benefit.

He threw open the door and they got out, Penny joining them. Mikko rounded the back of the car and leaned against the trunk. Gun in hand.

"Dude, we're in the middle of no-man's-land. Why the piece?" The weight of Elijah's Glock pressed against his spine, hidden by his coat.

Mikko tilted his head, wearing a quizzical expression. Had Elijah blown it? Several long seconds ticked by.

Penny laughed, a cackling noise akin to nails on a chalkboard. Elijah swung to look at her. "You're so funny, G. You know Mikko's Sig is like a pacifier. He always has it with him."

Tiandra joined in the taunting. "Maybe you got whacked harder on the head than we thought."

Elijah shrugged. "Whatever."

Mikko smiled, waving the gun. "This is why I had to talk to you together. You two know stuff. You're ahead of the curve."

Tiandra didn't flinch even with the Sig aimed at her.

"You're smart." Mikko shook his head. "I can't have loose cannons in my group. Gotta ensure the team is tight before the deal." He lifted the weapon as if inspecting it, then lowered the barrel and focused on them. "It's time to make a change."

Tiandra's heart drummed in her ears so loudly she barely heard Mikko. What was he rambling about? His eccentric ways and nonsensical speech confused her. She'd forgotten to tell Elijah that Mikko always kept the Sig Sauer close. But the shooters had gone after his car in the alley, and if he'd intended to kill her and Elijah, why rescue them? The wild look in Mikko's eyes indicated he was inebriated. *Great.*

She gripped Bosco's leash with one hand tightly beside her. He tensed, though that wasn't new. Her K-9 instinctively smelled scumbags when he met them. But he wouldn't respond without her orders. She shifted her feet and turned slightly, attempting a bored position while maneuvering her left hand toward her waistband, out of Mikko's sight. From her peripheral, she also spotted Elijah's right arm slide toward his weapon. Penny was too close. If he drew the gun, she'd see it and warn Mikko. Elijah twisted to conceal the Glock. Clearly, he worried this situation was about to go wrong.

Mikko continued rambling, making little sense about friendship and honor. Two things she doubted the Kings' leader understood. "Lots of fools wanna act like Kings," Mikko said, "but they don't have the guts to live the life."

Elijah grunted agreement. Tiandra remained silent.

"You sure about this?" Mikko asked, facing Penny.

"Positive. After everything we found out." Penny met Tiandra's gaze with a strange smile. "They've earned it."

Tiandra swallowed, her glance flicking to Bosco. Could she order him to run away and free him in time if Mikko shot at them?

"What's that?" Elijah asked.

Mikko chortled, then abruptly silenced. He paced in front of them.

Should Tiandra pull her weapon? Was the Op over?

Her fingers lingered on the handle of her Glock, ready to draw the gun.

Mikko stepped closer to her, standing within an inch of her face.

"Hey, man," Elijah began.

"Shh." Mikko quieted Elijah like a child. To his credit, Elijah didn't react. "I lost my friends. Vito and Orlando were my brothers. I don't take their loss lightly." Mikko's dark, venomous stare sent a chill down Tiandra's back. "I'll make sure whoever took them out pays. An eye for an eye, right?"

Tiandra refused to move her gaze away from Mikko. "Of course."

"I'm trying to figure out what happened. How they got in the line of fire from the Locos. Did someone set them up?"

"How would I know?" Tiandra snapped. "You got enemies too?"

Mikko tilted his head like a dog discerning a command. "Who doesn't?"

Tiandra remained stoic. "Then we're all in danger."

"Exactly. We need reinforcements."

Elijah stepped closer to her. "Dude, what's the point of this?"

"That's why we gotta talk face-to-face, to tell if you're lying." He lifted a hand, silencing Elijah, gaze on Tiandra.

Elijah's jaw flexed, and she worried he'd punch Mikko. She remained prepared to draw her Glock.

Finally, Mikko stepped back, apparently satisfied with whatever he saw or didn't see in their eyes. "I need insiders. People I can trust to make sure the deal goes down. With my guys being attacked, I wonder if someone's playing me. Setting me up for the 29 Locos Cartel."

Tiandra flicked a glance at Penny, who was clearly also inebriated. As if confirming Tiandra's suppositions, Penny teetered, steadying herself on the door.

"I need you two to be my eyes and ears." Mikko swung the Sig between Tiandra and Elijah. "I'm pulling you into the fold."

"That's an honor!" Penny exclaimed, clapping wildly.

Mikko grinned but it held no amusement, just evil. "Understand, if I find out you're two-faced, I'll shoot you dead where you stand." He again lifted his gun, gesturing toward them, then laughed a little too loudly. "Your mutt too. Not that I have anything against him, right, buddy?" Mikko leaned down to pet Bosco.

Tiandra tightened the leash with a soft shushing sound, fearing he'd bite Mikko. Most people instinctively understood not to get into a dog's face, but Mikko wasn't the sharpest pencil in the box, as her mother would say. Her hand remained poised behind her back, ready to draw her gun.

"We got this." Elijah's confident tone and strong posture indicated he'd embraced the role.

"Just remember, you're on probation. One wrong move..." Mikko rose again, meeting Tiandra's eyes. "There's no second chances." He pressed the Sig against her temple.

She refused to flinch. The creep loved intimidating people, but she wouldn't give him the satisfaction of cowering. Tiandra lifted her chin defiantly. "We're faithful to the cause." No lie there. "What makes you think we're not trustworthy?" She hated the hint of a quiver in her voice as she battled for self-control.

"You're good. For now. But that could change, right?" Mikko smirked. "Penny says you're the real deal. Are you?"

Elijah and Tiandra shared a glance. This was it—the break they needed. They'd finally get the details and takedown the Kings.

"We're totally in," Elijah responded.

"Yes!" Mikko waved the gun a little too emphatically, then lifted it and shot out into the ravine. The pops echoed in the night air. "Let's head back and make the big announcement to the Kings. It's good for the ranks to know their place in the hierarchy."

Penny raced to Tiandra and pulled her into a hug. "This is so great! We're like real sisters now."

The word penetrated her heart, reminding her of her older sister Meghan's last text message, asking Tiandra to call. The fighting, the distance, all of it seemed so insignificant. Family was precious, and she wanted to reunite with hers and grieve Anissa's loss together to keep her memory alive. Tiandra made an internal vow to make peace with Meghan as soon as the case was over.

"You okay?" Penny slurred her words.

"Yep." Tiandra released her Glock and lowered her arm, careful not to draw attention to the movement. They were in, and the deal was going down.

EIGHT

Elijah's phone pinged, waking him from sleep. He jerked upright, mentally kicking himself for allowing his body to rest. He glanced around the cramped room, hating the smell and the accommodations. The bed across from him supported a hulky man with so many piercings he'd never make it through a metal detector. He snored with such velocity, Elijah was certain he'd inhale the bedding. How had he fallen asleep with that racket?

The phone pinged again, reminding him of why he'd awakened. His roommate snorted before returning to his rhythmic log sawing. Elijah studied the screen, lit up by a text message from Tiandra.

Meet ASAP.

Elijah threw his legs over the bed, grateful he hadn't bothered to remove his boots. Based on the clock on his phone, he'd gotten four hours of sleep. *Joy.* But it had to be enough to keep him at the top of his game. He slipped from the room and moved down the hallway toward the steps. Descending, he passed quietly behind three gang members crashed out on the couches in front of the TV. The Kings lived like a college sorority, trading academic excellence for criminal activity.

One man shifted, knocking an object off the coffee table with his boot. Elijah whirled, aiming for the back door, and slipped out undetected.

He scurried across the lawn, where just hours prior, he and Tiandra had fought for their lives against a maniac with a crossbow. Several arrows still littered the yard. Normally, he'd have called the police to report the incident, but the Kings wouldn't invite law enforcement into their home regardless of the circumstances. They took care of justice on their own terms, which left a long line of destruction in their path.

He rounded the detached two-car garage and found Tiandra waiting beside a black SUV Mikko had provided for them after embracing them into his inner sanctum. An outward expression of his devotion for their service to the cause, as he'd referred to the generous offer. Whatever, the ride was supreme.

Wordlessly, he climbed inside the already running vehicle and snapped on his seat belt. The interior was warm and inviting. Tiandra pulled away from the house.

"So why this mysterious departure?"

"Read the text message from Penny." Tiandra gestured to her device, charging on the dash.

Elijah picked up the phone and read the text. T, I'm scared.

Tiandra's response. What's wrong?

I think I'm in danger. Please come over. Now.

Where's Mikko?

Dunno. No answer.

On my way.

"That's it? No reason?" Elijah asked.

"I wonder if it's just drugged paranoia."

"Does she do this often?"

"Penny's talented at overdramatization. Which explains why Mikko is ghosting her. She's a lot." Tiandra turned onto a side road. "However, she's my link. You saw how much she played into Mikko trusting us to take Vito and Orlando's place in the group."

"Yeah, even though he treats her badly, he seems to value her input," Elijah said.

"Which works great for us," Tiandra added.

"And it goes to show how well you've done in establishing the relationship with her. You got skills." Elijah gave her a one-handed fist bump.

"Thanks." Tiandra smiled.

He wanted to be the reason she smiled all the time. He blinked. Clearly, he needed sleep. His brain was wonky.

"Any problems getting out of the house?" Tiandra asked.

"Nope, they were all passed out."

"Good."

"I still can't remember everyone's names," Elijah confessed.

"No worries, they won't question you. Now that Mikko's made it known you're in the circle of trust or whatever he calls it, they'll respect you. You could call them all Doofus and they'd answer with, 'sir, yes, sir!'" Tiandra offered a mock salute. "Okay maybe not that bad, but you get the idea."

"I'd probably better hold off on any name-calling since they're always packing," Elijah gave a short laugh. "You were right. The hideout is not relaxing. I hate being stuck in there with them."

"Mikko wants someone to watch over the crew. So, you're welcome," Tiandra teased. "Thanks for making an excuse for me to travel for supplies in Rapid City, so I'd have a night away from them."

"It worked well. Still can't believe he bought the reason."

"In all fairness, when you suggested it, his inebriated state contributed to the approval."

"Timing is everything." Elijah winked. They'd needed a break to allow HFTF to scan the SUV for any tracking and listening devices.

"If it makes you feel better, Bosco and I didn't sleep much at the motel either."

"At least you're not stuck in a room with a guy who snores so loud, it sounds like a truck motor."

"You've obviously never been around Bosco when he's super tired." She chuckled.

At her words, the canine leaned over the console and nudged Elijah's arm. "Hey, buddy, I missed you too."

He stroked the dog's chin and marveled at how natural it felt to be with Tiandra. As though they belonged together. He quickly shoved aside the thoughts. *Focus, man.*

Tiandra pulled up to a run-down bungalow and parked in front of the sidewalk.

"Doesn't appear anyone's home," Elijah replied, surveying the property without lights glowing from inside.

"She hangs out in her bedroom usually, so that's not abnormal."

"Hmm, something seems off." Elijah reached for his Glock, checking the magazine.

Tiandra did the same. "Let's go in prepared."

They exited the SUV, Bosco leashed beside her, and approached the door.

Tiandra knocked, Elijah standing off to the side so he wasn't visible from the front window. "Hey, Penny, it's me."

Several minutes passed without a sound.

Tiandra rapped three more times. No response. She shot a worried glance at him. "This isn't right."

"Let me go first." They traded places, and he reached for the knob, turning it. "Unlocked."

They both withdrew their guns and held them in the ready position as they crossed the threshold. "Penny, it's Tia and G."

Tiandra flipped on the light switch. A single free-standing brass lamp illuminated the compact living room. The cleanliness and neatness of the home surprised Elijah. Throw pillows embroidered with fun sayings gave the old, stained couch and chair a homey appeal.

They walked through the space, Tiandra calling for Penny while Bosco sniffed a path.

They crossed the meager living room in four strides, passing the empty bathroom.

"Penny? It's Tia," Tiandra called.

No response.

Elijah ducked through a doorway beside the kitchen and peered inside, where a queen-size bed—made and neat—and narrow dresser filled the room. A white wrought-iron headboard and quilt gave the space a farmhouse appeal. He checked the closet and found clothes hanging neatly.

"She's not here." Elijah exited the bedroom, proceeding through an archway that opened to the larger kitchen, common for houses built in that era.

"My grandmother had a similar house." Elijah whispered. "She said kitchens back in the day were the biggest room because that's where families gathered before television became the American household idol."

Tiandra nodded from where she and Bosco stood next to a pantry door. "Your grandma and mine would've gotten along very well." She strolled to the living room and paused beside a framed picture on a side table. "Look at this." Tiandra lifted the frame and passed it to him.

Elijah moved closer, studying what appeared to be a family photo. A young girl with pigtails wore a pink dress and black Mary Jane shoes. She held the hand of a teen boy who wore dark pants, a button-down shirt, and tie. The father, mother, and grandmother all wore Sunday best clothing and big smiles.

"Is that Penny?" Elijah asked, pointing to the girl.

"Possibly." Tiandra studied the photo. "They appear happy." She returned the frame to the table.

"Wonder what changed."

They made another pass of the house, then met in the kitchen. Elijah rounded the rectangular farm table, passing a gas stove and outdated appliances on the far wall. He glanced out the large window over the sink, framed by tied-back white curtains, and looked into the backyard. "There's no one here."

"That's strange." Tiandra held her phone to her ear. "She's not answering."

Bosco walked toward the stove, sniffed, then barked three times. He stepped backward and barked again.

"What's he doing?" Elijah asked.

"We need to go," Tiandra said. "Now!"

"What about Penny?"

"She's not here. Mikko finally answered her and picked her up?"

"Possibly."

They rushed outside, wasting no time. They neared the SUV and Bosco barked three times again. He jerked Tiandra toward the street. Elijah jogged beside her, glancing over his shoulder just as Penny's house exploded into flames.

Tiandra landed hard on the road, ears ringing. Elijah toppled next to her, and though he moved his lips, she couldn't hear him. She shook her head.

He assisted Tiandra to stand while Bosco paced beside them, panting. Her knee ached and the shoulder she'd injured in the car accident throbbed as badly as it once had. They loaded into the SUV, which had sustained minor damage from the blast, and raced from the house.

"Are you okay?" Elijah's muffled voice pierced through the fogginess.

Tiandra groaned, shifting in the seat and holding her arm. "Yeah, that reactivated my injury from the car accident."

"Did Penny set us up?" Anger lingered in his tone.

"I wondered the same thing." Tiandra glanced at the road. "Um, where are you going?"

"Just trying to get away. Do you think she's at Mikko's house?"

"Hold up. Pull over and let me try her again."

Elijah did as Tiandra asked, and she activated the speakerphone. The line rang four times and went straight to voice mail. Elijah withdrew his cell and called Mikko, placing the call on speaker. Mikko answered on the third ring, sounding very much asleep. "What?"

"Penny's house just exploded and about took us with it." Elijah's voice was thick with accusation.

"Why were you at her place?" Mikko barked.

"She texted Tia—" Elijah halted at Tiandra's shaking head.

"What? No way." Mikko's slurred speech showed his inebriated status. "She's right here with me. Has been all night." He guffawed. "Dude, she's three sheets to the wind."

That coincided with her intoxicated state when they'd met with Mikko earlier in the evening. Penny had never texted Tiandra with a message like that before. Something didn't sit well, but she wouldn't discuss it with Mikko.

Based on Elijah's confused expression, he too had concerns. They needed to work the angle. Tiandra mouthed, *Ask him if the Locos are responsible.*

Elijah nodded. "Dude, did 29 Locos set us up to go there before torching the place?"

Mikko grunted. "Can't say it's 'mpossible." His slurred words blended.

"Somebody's working hard to kill us," Elijah said.

"Yeah, you should watch your back." Mikko

yawned loudly. "But whoever tried to hurt my Penny better beware." He hung up.

Tiandra shifted in the seat again, trying to find a comfortable position.

"Hmm, something's not right," Elijah said.

"Two things bother me. Whoever texted me from Penny's phone knows she and I are friends. Is someone surveilling us, or is the killer a part of the Kings?"

"If that was the case, wouldn't they already have us made?" Elijah argued.

"And if they discovered our identities, they'd hand us over to Mikko." Tiandra contemplated. "The second thing is Penny's never done that before. Texted me when she's with Mikko or inebriated."

"Someone accessed her phone remotely," Elijah surmised.

"And that implies a tech savvy killer."

"We should notify the team."

"Agreed." Tiandra dug into her combat boot and withdrew the task force cell phone. She typed a quick message. Need to meet ASAP.

The response came within seconds. Boathouse.

"Head south and watch for tails."

"Roger that." Elijah did a U-turn in the middle of the road, then accelerated.

Tiandra provided him directions, and they made record time getting to the vacated lake boathouse. "Pull in."

Skyler's SUV was parked inside, where she and Walsh waited.

Tiandra and Elijah exited the vehicle, and she released Bosco.

Skyler hurried forward. "You look like you got hit by a bus."

"Something like that." Tiandra provided a synopsis of the explosion. "We were definitely lured there."

"By whom?" Skyler asked.

"Good question." Tiandra leaned against the SUV grill. "Whoever wanted us dead could've handled that at the hideout or with me at the motel. Nothing makes sense."

"We'll have Eliana do a trace on Penny's cell phone," Walsh said, already tapping a text message to their tech guru.

"Mikko and Penny were blitzed when we dropped them off. I don't think either had the wherewithal to make a call or set that up tonight," Elijah added.

Walsh stood taller, crossing his arms over his chest. "This is getting too dangerous. We're withdrawing from the Op."

"No way!" Tiandra's reply came out harsher than she'd intended. "Sir, with all due respect..."

"I hate that lead-in," Walsh grumbled.

Tiandra inhaled. "Sir, we can't walk away now. Aside from the drug deal, which could kill hundreds, if not thousands, of innocent people, Graham's and Elijah's lives depend on identifying and apprehending whoever ordered the hit."

Walsh ran a hand over his head. "I know. I know."

"Are there any updates on my brother?" Elijah asked.

Skyler frowned. "Nothing has changed."

"I'm worried this is all going to go south, and I can't risk losing you both," Walsh contended.

"If we bail on the Op, that's already a reality," Tiandra argued. "Whether it's me or Elijah or he and Graham, whoever is out to kill us will make sure they get what they want."

"And my brother's attacker goes unpunished," Elijah added. "I'm with Tiandra on this. We must finish. We're up for the challenge."

Tiandra studied him. He resembled his brother in many ways, but in that moment, he did a complete 180-degree turn. Instead of asking Walsh to remove her from the case, he'd joined her in the fight to stay in the mission. That meant more to Tiandra than Elijah would ever understand.

"Let's play this out," Skyler said, redirecting the conversation. "What if Penny's in the killer's crosshairs?"

Tiandra spun to face her teammate. "You think she's in danger? Just like she said in the text?"

"What if her intoxicated state released her hidden fears?" Skyler asked. "Until that moment, she'd told no one."

"Sky, you're brilliant." Tiandra nodded. "That's plausible. If the attacker who set the bomb wasn't aware that Penny hadn't gone home, he wouldn't expect us to go there."

"They'd scheduled the bomb to detonate in the dead of night," Elijah added. "They were after Penny."

"I'll ensure crews gather evidence ASAP," Walsh said.

"We'll head to Mikko's in the morning." Tiandra glanced at Elijah, who chuckled. "Or afternoonish. They're not early risers."

"Good. Keep us updated, and watch your backs," Walsh ordered. "At the first sign you've been compromised—"

"We'll bounce," Elijah assured the commander.

NINE

Elijah leaned back in the dining room chair the next afternoon, stretching out his legs. His ankle had healed, leaving only a hint of soreness. Mikko sat beside him, rambling and flexing his ego muscles. The man's condescending treatment yet contrasting protectiveness of Penny intrigued Elijah. It was as though Mikko couldn't decide his role in the relationship. On the flip side, Penny remained the complacent girlfriend, unflinching at his inappropriate name-calling and callous jokes. Elijah couldn't figure them out, and he focused on surveying the house. Compared to Penny's modest and tidy home, Mikko's had gaudy decorations and posters on the walls, resembling a teenager's bedroom. They were complete opposites. Maybe that's what attracted them to each other.

Elijah's mind wandered, landing on Tiandra. How did she decorate her home? Did she have lots of pictures of her many siblings? Would they accept a guy like him?

"Right?" Mikko slapped Elijah's back hard, jolting him into the conversation.

Stifling the urge to throat punch the creep, Elijah offered a lame chuckle and tried to recall what Mikko had just said.

Penny and Tiandra sat on the sofa across the

room from him, talking easily and laughing. Bosco leaned against Tiandra, adoration in his expression. *Yeah, buddy, I totally understand. She's amazing.*

"Dude, that accident rattled your melon big time," Mikko guffawed.

"Why?" Elijah appeared bored, though his heart thudded. Had he messed up?

"You haven't taken your eyes off her all day." Mikko snorted. "She's hot. I get it."

Elijah chuckled nervously. As if overhearing Mikko, Tiandra glanced up, meeting Elijah's gaze, and smiled. She leaned down and said something to Bosco, who rose and strolled over to him and with a sigh, rested his head on Elijah's leg.

"Hmm, that's new too," Mikko said, lifting his drink. "You two bonded?"

Elijah tensed, determined to play off the questions. "Had to make peace with Tia, which meant getting along with him. She likes him more than me anyway."

Mikko laughed. "For real."

"Dogs are easier than women. A few bacon burgers and we're pals." He hoped Bosco wouldn't hold his words against him. "You know what they say. If Mama ain't happy—"

"Ain't nobody happy," Mikko chortled. "I know that's right." He threw his can of soda across the room, missing the trashbin by a mile. "Guess my NBA career is out of the question." He leaned back in his chair. "Penny! Get me another drink."

She shot to her feet and rushed to the kitchen, returning with a can. "Here, baby."

"Open it," he ordered.

Penny cracked the lid and passed it to Mikko, then returned to her seat by Tiandra.

Elijah sipped his energy drink, gently nudging Bosco under the table with his toe. The dog took the hint and reverted to Tiandra.

"Been thinking…" Mikko leaned closer. "Locos might go after Penny because she's mine."

"Got a plan?" Elijah asked.

"Of course."

"Good. Catch me up. When's the deal going down?"

Mikko worked his jaw, a flash of irritation snapping in his dark eyes. "You're on a need-to-know basis."

"How are we supposed to be watching out for you when you refuse to share info?" Elijah jerked his chin toward Penny, throwing down the gauntlet, and said, "Does she know?"

"What's it to you?" Mikko narrowed his dark eyes.

Elijah lowered his voice. "Is she playing both sides? Did she tell the Locos about the deal?"

"I'll ignore that question," Mikko growled.

He had damage control to do and fast or this conversation would spiral. Treading carefully with Mikko, Elijah whispered, "Hear me out. I got your back."

"Nah, she's loyal. She'd give her life for me," Mikko replied. "Why? You wonder the same about Tia betraying you?"

"I trust no one completely." Elijah shrugged. "If I thought Tia stabbed me in the back, though, I'd take care of the problem."

"Yeah. Same." Mikko sighed. "Thing is, I can't tell what I don't know." He paused, apparently realizing he'd spilled an important detail, and added, "Or what I don't want to say."

Elijah nodded, sipping the energy drink as understanding coursed through him. Mikko didn't have the deal date information, which meant his supplier didn't trust him with the details. Why? "So, you're not in the know either."

Mikko seemed to consider the comment. Probably challenging the finite brain matter drugs hadn't destroyed. "I don't question them. Take a lesson in there."

"No disrespect." Elijah lifted a hand in mock surrender. "Just keeping one eye open in this business."

"I have to trust someone. That's why I have you covering me." Mikko sighed and settled in his chair. "Should I kick Tia to the curb?"

Elijah's plan had swerved into dangerous territory. "I got it handled. She's cool."

"All right. You've made your point and I appreciate the honesty. I'll keep Penny extra close from here on out." He stood. "Penny! Get over here."

Faster than Bosco would respond to Tiandra's order, Penny raced to Mikko's side. He snaked an arm around her waist and pulled her closer. "You stay beside me from here on out. Don't talk to no one." He gave Elijah a jerk of his chin. "Not even G or Tia unless we're in the room together."

"Aw, not even Tia?" Penny whined. "She's my homegirl."

"Nope. Not unless I'm in the room."

"Okay." Penny nodded, her face forlorn.

Great, what had he done? Tiandra was making headway, and he'd just cut off that line of communication.

Tiandra sauntered toward them, wearing a quizzical expression. "What's up?"

"From now on, you and Penny only talk in my presence," Mikko answered.

Tiandra shot Elijah a confused look. "Why?"

"Because I said so!" Mikko thundered.

Elijah reached for Tiandra, pulling her into a sideways hug. Her body stiffened, but she complied. "He's watching out for her."

"Like you do for me, huh?" Tiandra cooed, playing into the situation. "Good thing Penny was here with you last night. Otherwise, she'd be dead."

"Excellent point." Suspicion hovered in Mikko's tone.

"We've got your back, Mikko," Tiandra added.

"Guess we'll see." His gaze toggled between the women. "There's no room at the hideout tonight."

Elijah shrugged. "No sweat." He stood. "We better bounce. And leave these two lovebirds alone."

They exited the house, walking to the SUV, when Penny raced outside. "Wait! Tia, you left this." She handed Tiandra her leather jacket.

Elijah moved to the front of the vehicle, listening in.

"Don't mind Mikko. He's bad at showing his feelings, especially when he's worried about me. He's so protective." Penny hugged Tiandra. "Do you need a place to stay?"

"Don't worry about me. Bosco and I are cool." Tiandra smiled and loaded the K-9 as Penny scurried to the house, waving once before closing the door.

Once they were seated, she asked, "What happened back there?"

"I stuck my size eleven boot in my mouth." Elijah replayed the conversation for Tiandra, including Mikko's slipup about not having the drug deal details. "I'm sorry. My mother always told me to pray before I speak. She recommended spiritual duct tape."

Tiandra giggled. Her gaze held his. "It's all good. You have no reason to be sorry. You're working the case."

"I must've hit a nerve with Mikko." Elijah shook his head. "Lord, give me wisdom to keep myself out of trouble," he prayed aloud.

"Amen for both of us. Honestly, it's not a bad

thing to poke the bear." Tiandra tapped her fingers on the dashboard. "Actually, not a bad thing at all."

"How do you figure?"

"Your conversation got Mikko hot under the gang-leader collar. He's circling the SUVs, so to speak. To protect her, Mikko's refusing to let Penny have her own life."

"Or he's afraid she'll accidentally tell us something. He got his hackles up when I asked about whether Penny knew anything about the deal."

"Do you think he lied? Is he worried she'll tell me his secrets?" Tiandra groaned. "Ugh. I was so close."

Elijah gripped the steering wheel. He'd failed big time. How would he fix this with Mikko? Though Tiandra didn't say it, he felt guilty. He'd talked too much and closed the door they'd just opened.

"Nope. We're not giving up." Tiandra addressed his internal quandary. "The real enemy is whoever paid the assassin to kill you."

"Does that person want something from me, are they preventing me from getting something, or do they believe I have something they want?"

"Play it out."

"Graham said he'd found an insider, right?" Elijah asked.

"Yes."

"Maybe that's the payer. Or is it a 29 Locos Cartel member trying to eliminate me because he thinks I can identify him?"

"Both are viable options."

Tiandra reached into her boot and withdrew the task force cell phone, placing the call on speakerphone.

Eliana answered. "Hey, you're stuck with me since everyone's out of the office."

"You're the brains behind the technical ops anyway. It's better for me to talk with you."

"Shh, don't tell," Eliana teased.

Tiandra chuckled. "Elijah and I are tackling this from another angle. Have you discovered any new leads from the accident?"

"No, Graham's motorcycle was mangled. We're still trying to extract evidence, but it's akin to untying a pretzel."

"What about the insider Graham mentioned?"

"Nope," Eliana said. "Walsh and Skyler are working hard, but Graham didn't provide notes or information to get us started. Wish he'd told you what he'd found before crashing—"

"Right," Tiandra cut her off. "Thanks anyway. Please let us know if you find anything."

"Will do."

They disconnected, and Tiandra faced him. "I'm sorry. Riker's candid speech has apparently worn off on Eliana. We'd hoped it would go the other way around."

"No worries, I'd rather deal with the truth," Elijah replied. "What're your thoughts about Graham's bike?"

"There's always evidence somewhere. We just need to find it."

"I agree," Elijah said. "And unfortunately, I think the assassin assumes the same."

Morning sunlight sliced through the gap between the cheap motel curtains. Tiandra rolled over, rubbing her eyes. Bosco snored seamlessly, taking up most of the bed. She chuckled and threaded her fingers through his soft fur. Somehow, she'd learned to tune him out in order to sleep. That was a serious life skill she'd apply to her resume.

Tiandra reached for her phone. No messages or calls had interrupted her overnight, giving her the first full night's rest since her hospital stay. Her thoughts traveled to Elijah. How had he done at the hideout? Poor guy.

She lay on her back staring at the ceiling, struggling to reconcile the Graham/Elijah complexities. Elijah's apologies for possibly upsetting Mikko had thrown her off. When had Graham apologized for anything, ever? Elijah's humility added to his already physical attractiveness. His identical appearance to her injured partner—whom she still had issues with—confused her. It was like dealing with a Jekyll and Hyde scenario. She reminded herself Elijah and Graham were separate individuals.

No, Elijah was not Graham.

And that's what scared her.

He even prayed, out loud, unprompted. Graham

prayed with the team, but Elijah's faith seemed different. Straightforward. No pretense, no outward show. Real. Authentic. They needed to finish this Op fast because the more time she spent with Elijah, the harder it was to ignore how much she enjoyed his company.

Bosco rolled over and yawned, emitting a soft squeak as he stretched his legs and flexed his paws upward.

"Good morning," Tiandra cooed, scratching his belly. "I see, standard kill position," she teased. "Come on, let's go outside."

She threw off the covers and slipped out of the bed, glimpsing her reflection in the skinny wall mirror. When was the last time she'd slept in pajamas and not her outfit from the day before? She slid her feet into her boots and donned her coat and gloves.

Bosco hopped down and joined her at the door, allowing Tiandra to snap on his leash.

With a peek out of the corner of the curtain to ensure it was safe, they stepped outside. Tiandra sucked in a breath, momentarily caught off guard by the freezing wind that greeted her. "Let's make this quick," she said, closing the locked door behind her.

They meandered to the copse of trees across the parking lot, allowing Bosco privacy. Tiandra continually scanned her surroundings, another habit she'd developed while working undercover. She never took for granted that the assassin might follow them.

Her thoughts bounced around in random order, somehow settling on Elijah, as they often did lately.

Had he slept in? She'd expected him to text as soon as he'd awakened. If he'd finally gotten some sleep, she didn't want to wake the poor guy.

She glanced at her cell phone. It was still early. She'd wait another hour before bothering him.

Bosco completed his business, and they walked back to the motel. Though the air was crisp, the bright sun invigorated her.

Tiandra entered her room then locked and closed the door. "Bosco, how about a morning run?"

He thumped his tail against the mattress, mouth parted in an expression resembling a grin.

She changed into cold gear leggings, a hoodie, and running shoes. Then she put Bosco's halter on, and slid the connecting leash around her waist, freeing her hands.

They headed outside for the second time and jogged through the parking lot to the adjoining sidewalk. The sun the day before had melted some of the snow, but she steered clear of icy patches, maintaining a light pace. The physical effort reinvigorated her body, but her mind refused to relax. Instead, her thoughts returned to Elijah.

Even Bosco had taken a liking to him, although she'd not missed Mikko's comment about Bosco and Elijah's newfound friendship. That was something she'd worried would become an issue. Mikko had picked up on the difference, and they couldn't ignore those types of nuances. She owned that mistake since the responsibility of predicting those possibilities rested on her shoulders as the seasoned undercover officer. Tiandra concluded upping her game was necessary from here forward.

He'd done a great job of diverting the situation with Mikko. Tiandra couldn't help but compare the twins again. Graham would've never commented about making her happy. That just wasn't his style.

Convinced any woman Elijah cared for would be treated with special care, Tiandra frowned. Would she ever know that kind of love? The thought saddened her. How would marrying someone like him change her life? Everything about Elijah Kenyon was good.

Too good. And she couldn't think that way about him.

"Get a grip," she huffed under her breath, increasing her pace.

Tiandra prayed the rest of the run, focusing on Graham's healing, the mission, and staying her mind on course. By the time she finished the five miles, her body was tired and her resolve reinvigorated. She hurried to shower and dress, then checked her text messages. Still nothing. A glance at the clock and a sudden ravenous hunger had Tiandra determined to wake Elijah.

Good morning.

His delayed response worried her. Finally, a message pinged through.

Sorry. Phone under the bed.

Rise and shine.

Ugh.

That bad?

Better now.

She smiled. Breakfast? I'm starving.

Same. On it.

Tiandra finished getting ready when she was startled by a knock on the door. Bosco barked his reply, and she silenced him with an upright hand. She grabbed her Glock, keeping it in her right hand, then peered out of the peephole. A young man stood on the other side, holding a foam cup and a small paper bag. He glanced over his shoulder at the jalopy behind him, sporting a familiar food delivery service logo magnet on the hood.

Elijah's text bounced to the forefront of her mind. *On it.* Had he ordered food to be delivered?

"Hurry up," the delivery guy whined.

Tiandra carefully cracked open the door, concealing the gun.

"Here ya go." The delivery driver shoved the bag and cup at her.

Tiandra gripped them in one hand, trying not to let the items fall to the ground. "I didn't order anything."

"Not my problem. I just deliver." He spun on his heel, obviously in a rush to get to his next destination.

"Okay, let me grab my purse," she called.

"Already paid for," he said over his shoulder, sliding behind the wheel.

Tiandra glanced at the bag where a note in permanent marker read, *Start without me.* How sweet of Elijah. She set down the items, then filled Bosco's food and water bowls, placing them on the floor.

She smiled at Elijah's thoughtfulness as she dropped onto the chair at the circular table and peered inside the bag. A sausage croissant. The delicious aroma of that and the hot coffee wafted to her. She sipped the drink. Mocha. Her favorite. Tiandra took a small bite of the sandwich, relishing the savory meat and cheese combination.

After consuming half of the meal, Tiandra's stomach tightened with severe cramps. She yelped, gripping her midsection.

She stood, teetering and steadied herself on the table, which rocked against her weight.

Bosco whined, head tilted in concern.

Tiandra couldn't speak against the acute pain.

The room spun, and nausea consumed her. Saliva filled her mouth, and she rushed past the table, aiming for the bathroom. She clung to the walls, chair, and dresser for support on the way, colliding with each piece as she stumbled to the toilet.

Finally, she reached the commode and fell to her knees.

Bosco hurried beside her, licking her face.

Though she wanted to reassure him she was okay, the pain in her head and stomach was so intense it immobilized her. After releasing her breakfast, she placed her head on the cold porcelain and with one hand dug into her boot for the task force cell phone. Her hands shook and after several attempts, she pried the device loose.

Another round of cramps overwhelmed her, and Tiandra cried out, clutching her stomach. With the phone still in hand, she twisted to lay her head on the linoleum floor. The cold soothed her face against the heatwave coursing through her body.

Tiandra could scarcely breathe. She glanced sideways, lifting the cell to read the numbers. In her peripheral vision, she got another peek at the table where the mostly consumed meal sat.

Realization battled with her body's desperate need to fight through the pain.

Tiandra blinked.

A single thought crashed through her conscious. Poison.

She again tried to lift the phone, but her arm felt weighted, dragging her hand down to the floor. Another pulsing cramp took her breath away.

Then the strangest sensation consumed Tiandra and she fell deep into blackness.

TEN

Elijah pulled into the motel parking lot, squinting against the bright morning sunlight. His roommate had sawed a forest full of logs the night before, keeping him awake. How did the man sleep through his own snoring?

He parked the SUV in front of Tiandra's room and slid from behind the wheel. Breakfast sounded good and a caffeine boost was necessary.

Bosco peered from the corner of the window curtain, scratching at the glass in rapid, frantic moves.

"Bosco?" Elijah rapped on the door while surveying the area. A few old beaters littered the aged motel's parking lot, familiar from Elijah's prior trips. "Tia, it's me," he said, using her undercover name.

Concern wove through him as Bosco barked and scratched at the window. Elijah stepped to the side and rushed the door, crashing into it with all his strength. After two more slams to the structure, the lock gave, and the door swung open. Bosco bolted outside, barking, then turned and ran to where Tiandra's body lay in the bathroom. Outstretched, her right hand clung to her task force phone. Elijah rushed to her and knelt, checking for a pulse. He exhaled relief at the slight movement beneath his fingertips. He took the phone from her open palm and called 9-1-1.

"9-1-1, what's your emergency?" the operator asked in a too calm voice.

"Send an ambulance to the River Edge Motel room 3 near the Whistler Gulch Campground."

"What's—"

Elijah hung up, not waiting for the operator's reply, then dialed the team.

"Where—"

"Tiandra's hurt!" Elijah cut off Walsh's question. "Maybe poisoned. Looks like she vomited and there's a fast-food bag on the table."

"Sending help."

"I called 9-1-1," Elijah said.

"Good. We'll send reinforcements."

"What about our cover?"

"I'll handle it. Stay with her."

As though Elijah would go anywhere else. "Do I give them her real name?"

"No! Maintain your cover, and keep this phone hidden on you until you hear from me again. We'll meet you at the hospital."

"Roger that."

Elijah tucked the cell into his pocket. He grabbed the washcloth from the shower and gently wiped Tiandra's mouth. Her flawless skin was pasty, damp, and blanched whiter than his mother's best guest towels. He helped Tiandra to lie more comfortably on her side. Bosco waited with them, whining soulfully.

"You saw it all, didn't you, buddy?"

The dog's eyes pleaded for help.

"They're coming. She'll be okay." Elijah cradled Tiandra against his chest. "I'm here. Hold on. Please hold on."

Her head was damp with perspiration, and her breaths remained shallow.

Elijah prayed harder than he'd ever had in his life.

At last, sirens screamed in the distance, growing louder and closer.

The Malinois spun, his hackles raised.

"Stay, Bosco." Elijah grasped the dog's collar with one hand. "That's help."

"Paramedics," a man's voice called out from the front door, eliciting the K-9's barked response.

"Is your dog secure?"

"Yes, he's fine. We're here in the bathroom!" Elijah hollered, though he could see the man approaching from where he sat.

The paramedic gave him a wary look, no doubt intimidated by the Malinois's presence. Elijah was stuck, unable to let go of Tiandra or the dog.

"Sir, you must secure your animal so I can help the patient."

Elijah reluctantly released Tiandra, gently slipping out from under her, and lifted Bosco into a cradled position in his arms.

He shifted to the side, giving the medics room to work, and watched. Did Bosco's instincts tell him the medic was safe? Perhaps it was the uniform. No doubt the dog had been around law enforcement from day one and trusted those wearing the clothing.

Elijah sat on the edge of the bed, still holding Bosco as a second medic raced inside and rushed to Tiandra.

"Looks like she was eating and got sick," Elijah said. "Possibly poisoned?"

"What did your friend ingest?" the first asked.

"I don't know."

"Let's get her transported." The two men worked to load Tiandra onto a stretcher while Elijah watched helplessly as they wheeled her from the room.

The first hollered the name of the hospital, which Elijah barely computed as he followed them. A small crowd of curious onlookers had gathered outside the other motel doors. Any one of them could be 29 Locos Cartel or the paid assassin.

The task force phone buzzed in his pocket and Elijah set Bosco down beside him, ordering, "Stay."

The medics loaded Tiandra into the ambulance and activated the siren, exiting the scene. Elijah withdrew the phone. A text message ordered him to go to the hospital and advised him the team would take over the scene.

Elijah glanced up, spotting HFTF's Chance Tavalla in the distance wearing a baseball cap and puffer coat, looking like the average tourist. Their eyes met briefly, and Elijah averted his gaze, typing a response. Gather the food and coffee trash.

He tucked the phone into his pocket and loaded Bosco into the SUV and headed to the hospital, praying for Tiandra.

As he trailed the rig, Elijah's anger burned hot. Was Mikko responsible? He was aware of Tiandra's location. Elijah vowed to make whoever hurt Tiandra pay. They'd gone after his brother, and now they'd crossed the line by going after the woman he cared about.

And someone would answer for both.

Tiandra groaned. Her stomach ached with soreness as if she'd just completed a CrossFit workout. IV lines carried fluids to her hand. It felt like a déjà vu experience from the car accident.

But this time, instead of Skyler, Elijah sat beside her. "Hey." He scooted forward, perching on the end of the seat. His forehead creased and sadness hung in his stormy irises.

"What happened?" Tiandra croaked.

"I was hoping you'd tell me. The doctors say you had off the charts amounts of arsenic in your system."

"That explains the torturous pain."

"I'm so sorry for not being there to protect you. To stop whoever did this," Elijah blurted.

"What? This isn't your fault." Tiandra sucked in a breath. "It was in the delivery food." She scoured her mind, trying to recall the last memories before waking in the hospital room. "A young guy came to the door."

"Did you recognize him?"

"No. Practically a kid. He drove an old sedan with a food delivery chain magnet on the hood."

"Do you remember which one?"

Tiandra tried to picture it, but her mind was fuzzy. "It was bright yellow."

"Okay, I know the company you're talking about." Elijah nodded emphatically. "What else?"

"Nothing. He seemed impatient, like he was in a hurry. He shoved the food at me and took off." Tiandra struggled to swallow against the dryness in her mouth.

Elijah quickly grabbed the plastic cup off the side table and filled it with water from a clear pitcher.

He helped her to sit up and lifted the cup to her lips, allowing her to sip the liquid. The coolness quenched her parched and sore throat. "I just assumed you'd sent the food." She rested against the pillow.

Elijah tilted his head, quickly withdrew his cell phone, and groaned. "Because I said, 'on it'?"

"Yeah, and the words *start without me* were written on the bag."

"Wish I was that thoughtful." Elijah grasped her

free hand. "What scares me is that someone either read our messages or they took the opportunity."

"But why not just shoot me? Why poison?"

"That I cannot answer."

"Is Mikko aware?"

"Not yet." Elijah glanced down, working his jaw.

"What aren't you saying?" Tiandra pushed herself up. She winced against the tightness in her stomach. "I feel like I did a thousand sit-ups."

"You did a lot of vomiting," Elijah said.

She cringed. "Did you witness that?"

"No."

Relief coursed through her. "Well, that explains the pain."

"About Mikko… I waited to call him because I wanted you to listen in."

"Do it. Let's see if he's got any idea what happened."

Elijah raised his cell and put it on speakerphone.

The line rang twice, and Mikko answered. "Speak, freak."

Tiandra shook her head at the man's lack of couth.

"It's G," Elijah's baritone rumble left no room for niceties. "We've got a problem."

"Now what?" Mikko's blasé attitude oozed through the receiver.

"Someone tried to kill Tia." He met her eyes and Tiandra's heart squeezed at the vulnerability she saw there.

"When? How?" Mikko asked the right questions, but his bored tone indicated disinterest.

"This morning. Poison," Elijah said. "This is out of control. I'm not wasting a single second away from her. Find someone else to babysit the hideout."

"Careful. Sounds like you forgot who you're talking to."

Elijah worked his jaw and Tiandra shook her head and mouthed, *Keep cool.* "I'm just worried."

"I get it. After what happened to Penny, I want payback too."

"I can't stay at the hideout anymore," Elijah said. "I need to protect Tia."

Mikko sighed heavily. "Funny thing, I noticed all the danger seems to follow the two of you. That's becoming a bit of an issue."

"What're you saying?"

"I'm thinking," Mikko replied.

Elijah narrowed his eyes, waiting for Mikko's next words.

"You and Tia meet me at the Old Rusty Saloon tomorrow night."

"She's in the hospital. I don't know when they'll release her."

"All right, I'll come there," Mikko said. "Which one?"

That could go a couple different ways. If Mikko knew where she was, would he try to kill her again? She and Elijah held gazes for several long seconds as if silently communicating the concern.

"G!"

Tiandra nodded, and Elijah provided the hospital name.

"On my way."

They disconnected.

Elijah got to his feet and paced at the end of her bed. "That might've been a huge mistake. We just gave him access to you."

"Anything else would've increased his suspicions."

"Maybe he's thinking of removing us as his trusted advisors." Tiandra emphasized the last words with sarcasm.

"I hope not. He knew you were staying at the motel, and he has eyes watching me at the hideout," Elijah said. "He'd have firsthand knowledge of when I left if he's following us."

"Sure, it's feasible." Tiandra shifted and Elijah rushed to her side, adjusting her pillow and blankets. She smiled at him. "Thank you for being here."

"Where else would I be?" His question was sincere, soft, and thoughtful.

"Um, where's Bosco?" Tiandra diverted the conversation and glanced around the room.

"I took him to the vet."

Tiandra bolted upright, instantly regretting the move. "What? Was he hurt? Why didn't you start with that? What happened?"

Elijah rested a hand on her shoulder. "No. No."

He leaned closer. "He's at the Walsh Veterinary Clinic." He winked, and Tiandra's body melted with relief.

"Oh. You about gave me a heart attack," she grumbled.

"I had to make sure he was out of danger while you were here."

Tiandra's heart welled with appreciation for his thoughtfulness. "He's okay, though?"

"He watched and protected you. When I got to your room, he went ballistic trying to tell me you were sick. He's an amazing animal."

Tiandra's eyes welled with tears. "The best."

"When this is all said and done—provided I actually survive the mission—I'd like to certify as a K-9 handler."

Tiandra blinked. Graham never would've made that comment. "For real?"

"Yeah. I mean if you think I'm handler material?" Elijah returned to the chair, dragging it closer to Tiandra's bedside.

"The dogs are the brilliant ones. We just hold the leash." Tiandra smiled at him. "And I'll teach you a few things."

"Well, then, that's seals it. You're committed now." He chuckled. "Sioux City PD is always looking for opportunities to bring in K-9s."

Sorrow enveloped Tiandra's chest. He'd return to Iowa when the mission was over. How had she forgotten that important detail?

The door opened and Elijah whirled around, hand against his back where Tiandra knew he hid his gun.

A petite woman entered wearing light blue scrubs. Tiandra studied her. She held an iPad and walked with confidence. Her thick auburn hair swayed above her shoulders as she approached Tiandra. "I'm sorry, sir, but you'll have to step out so I can do my exam."

Elijah opened his mouth as though he intended to argue.

"It's okay," Tiandra assured him, glancing at the nurse's name tag where *Kristie* was printed in bold letters next to an ID picture of the woman standing before her. Something vaguely familiar about her resonated with Tiandra, but it didn't raise her fears. Rather, it was almost peaceful. Like the arrival of a friend.

"Glad to see you've returned to the living," Kristie said. "You probably don't remember me talking to you earlier. You were out of it."

The recollection of the woman speaking reassurances and praying for Tiandra bounced to the forefront of her mind. "I do. A little."

Kristie smiled.

Elijah's phone rang, and he glimpsed the screen then showed it to her. A text from Mikko. In the parking lot.

"Go," she assured. "It's fine."

"I'll be right back," he promised, stroking the

side of her cheek with his finger with such tenderness it nearly undid Tiandra's resolve.

She fought to maintain a neutral expression, though his touch sent a jolt of electricity through her like she'd never known before. Everything within her wanted to lunge into his arms. Instead, she gripped the sheet with both hands, fisting them in place.

"Go on, handsome," the nurse assured. "Nurse Kristie is here." The playfulness in the woman's tone lightened the mood, and Elijah smiled.

But his reluctant departure touched Tiandra.

The door closed softly behind him.

"Doc might release you in the morning," Kristie said, checking Tiandra's vitals. "Insurance doesn't allow you to stay long in the hospital," she added, entering data into the iPad. "The counter-meds are working well."

"That's great news," Tiandra said.

Kristie set the device on the side table. "I must ask this. Do you have any idea who might've done this to you?" She flicked a glance at the door.

"No." Tiandra shook her head. "But I plan to find out."

"If you're afraid for your safety…" She again looked at the door.

"Not of him," Tiandra assured her. "I trust him with my life."

The nurse nodded with a slight smile. "He hasn't left your side."

"Really?"

"Nope." Kristie moved around the bed, checking the IV machine. "Boyfriend?" She glanced at Tiandra's hand. "A guess because you're not wearing a ring."

To maintain her cover, she had to complete the ruse. But lying was so hard. It battled against everything Tiandra believed. Still, this was a role, a part she played. She had to do it well. Who knew how wide the Kings' nefarious reach went.

"He's pretty special," she answered honestly.

"And hot." Kristie winked.

Tiandra's neck warmed. "Yeah, that too." And so off-limits.

Except her heart argued that reasoning. Because Elijah Kenyon was everything Tiandra wanted and more. And that made him more dangerous to her than any arsenic-toting killer.

ELEVEN

"You cannot be serious. Tia and I are risking our lives to do the job you gave us." Elijah stood in front of Mikko, desperately wanting to grab the smug creep's throat and shake some sense into him. Mikko's threat to remove he and Tia from their promotions infuriated Elijah. Only the reminder that they had to complete the Op kept him from following through with that move.

"Don't know." Mikko gave an exaggerated sigh and shook his head. "You two find a lot of trouble."

"You told me there's a bull's-eye painted on my back," Elijah reminded the man. "And you made a public show the other night at the hideout by telling everyone that Tia and I are replacing Vito and Orlando."

Mikko's head shot up and he glared at Elijah. "Nobody replaces Vito and Orlando."

Elijah raised his hands in surrender. "It's a figure of speech."

"Uh-huh," Mikko grunted. "I'm just sayin' I've gotta rethink that promotion. What exactly happened to Tia?"

"Arsenic poisoning."

Mikko exhaled an expletive, and Elijah wasn't sure if it was from surprise or fear. He covered his mouth. "How?"

"Food delivery." Elijah pierced Mikko with a hard stare, searching for any signs of deception. "That's no coincidence. It was someone at the hideout."

"Be careful throwing out accusations like that."

"I'm only stating the obvious."

"Dude, you're flat out calling your brothers 'dirty.'"

"Maybe." Elijah couldn't help but ponder the irony of that statement, considering the Kings were involved in criminal activity. "What if one of them wants to be your number two? Was anyone else in line?"

"They all want that job." Mikko exhaled. "Never thought I'd lose Vito or Orlando." He paced a path in front of the Mercedes. "Yeah. Yeah. That's possible."

Somehow, Elijah had to pry the drug deal information from Mikko. "Tia and I are still in. Committed. Whoever is trying to take us out is failing. We're no quitters. You say when and where and we're there."

"When I find out, you will," Mikko replied coolly.

So Mikko was clueless. Great. That meant they'd have a last-minute notification to share with the task force. How would the team prepare for the takedown? He needed to talk to Tiandra fast.

"Are we good?" Elijah asked.

"Yeah. I s'pose."

"Cool. I gotta go back to Tia." He gave a shrug. "You know how it is. She'll be raging mad I've been gone so long." Elijah rolled his eyes for effect.

Mikko chuckled. "Yeah, I get that." He offered Elijah a fist bump. "Just remember, your allegiance is to me first. And if it isn't…well…that's a problem."

My allegiance is to God alone. "Not an issue."

Mikko tilted his head, giving him the appearance of a confused dog. Although Bosco's intelligence far exceeded Mikko's. Elijah suppressed a grin.

"Glad to hear it." Mikko tapped out a cigarette. "How long you been with me now?"

Elijah's pulse ratcheted, and his mind blanked. When had Graham and Tiandra gone undercover? Was this a test? "Since birth," he answered, flippantly.

Mikko snorted and blew out a slow breath. "You two will stay at my house. Better if we're all under the same roof when we get word the deal is going down."

"That's generous, but we couldn't impose." Elijah bit his lip, aware he sounded more like royalty than a street thug.

"Not an option," Mikko said, apparently nonplussed by the mistake. "Things are amping up for the deal. I want you available at a second's notice. Let me know when she's released."

"Cool." Elijah tucked his hands into his pockets. "I'll be in touch."

Though every cop instinct warred against Elijah turning his back on Mikko, he knew the action would demonstrate he trusted the man. *God, thank You for being my protector.*

He trekked across the parking lot and entered the hospital without looking over his shoulder. Once the elevator doors closed, Elijah exhaled the breath he didn't realize he'd held. Thoughts sped through his mind with rocket force. He and Tiandra had to brainstorm.

The elevator dinged, and the doors opened onto the fourth floor. The hallway lights had dimmed, reminding him of the late hour. Would they refuse to let him into Tiandra's room? He scurried past the empty nurses' station and through her door.

She sat in bed watching TV and smiled at his entrance. "Did they give you a hard time for being here after visiting hours?"

"They didn't see me," Elijah said. "Sorta ran straight to your room."

She chuckled. "Nice."

He nodded his head toward the window, indicating the outside. "That meeting was interesting."

"Yeah, what'd he want?"

Elijah dropped into the chair at Tiandra's bedside. "He's got no clue when the deal's happening."

"What? For real?"

"Nope. I figured he'd slipped earlier at the house,

but tonight confirmed it. Whoever his supplier is, they don't trust him with the details or they're keeping it on the down-low to avoid any leaks."

Tiandra shut off the TV. "I wonder who he's working with? They've obviously got power over him."

"Me too." He ran a hand over his hair. "What if they do a last-minute deal? How will HFTF get there in time?" He sat back in the seat, propping his leg over his knee.

"That'll be up to them to figure out. We have enough to cope with on this end." Tiandra leaned her head against the pillow.

Elijah wanted to thread his fingers through her long brown hair framing her face.

"The hard part is notifying them in time," she added.

"Exactly. Which brings me to the second issue."

"What's that?" Tiandra turned to him.

"Mikko wants us to stay at his house because he insists we need to be close when the deal goes down."

Her eyebrows furrowed. "Think he's made us?"

"No, but he's suspicious."

"Well, aren't you full of good news." Tiandra teased, though her eyes remained serious.

"That's me," Elijah quipped. "However, if we use that to our advantage, we might buy enough time to notify HFTF."

"Except that'll impede our ability to meet with the team."

"Now who's the one with good news?" Elijah stretched his arms overhead and closed his eyes. "What's our next step?"

"Update Walsh."

Elijah withdrew Tiandra's task force phone from his jeans pocket just as the door opened. He shoved the device from view and glanced up, spotting another nurse dressed in scrubs enter. He started to protest when she stepped closer.

"Sky!" Tiandra said in a whispered cheer.

"Hey, what's the latest?" Skyler sat on the edge of Tiandra's bed.

They quickly updated her.

"Guess you two will have to go dark," Skyler said. "But you understand the danger that puts you in without regular check-in times. We won't know if you're okay."

Tiandra gave Elijah a worried nod. "Right."

"You'll be in the enemy's lair," Skyler added as if that was new information. "Make sure you hide your task force cell phone well. Expect zero privacy."

"We were just discussing that." Elijah tucked away the phone. "How about the last-minute takedown once we have the date, time, and location?"

"Don't worry about that," Skyler reassured him. "We're locked and ready to load at the first notice."

Elijah was unconvinced. "But the distance to get here…"

"We're closer than you think." Skyler assured.

He grinned. "Oh, yeah, it was good seeing Chance at the motel this morning."

"No idea what you're talking about," Skyler said with a wink.

"Right, right. You're both figments of my imagination," Elijah jested.

Skyler got to her feet. "Stay safe. Keep us updated as you can. Stick with ten codes whenever possible to avoid leaving a trail." She referenced the police radio communication system.

"Roger that," Elijah said.

Skyler slipped out of the room.

"Yeah, I get why you do this," he said. "The adrenaline rush of danger and all, but it's stressful."

"Tell me about it."

"Mikko almost stumped me. Thought I was a gonner."

Tiandra quirked a brow. "Really? Why?"

"He asked how long we'd been in the Kings."

Tiandra rolled her eyes. "He's clueless, especially considering all the drugs he uses. Penny, however, would be a different conversation. And she's got his ear."

"How long has it been?"

"Ten months, three weeks, four days." Tiandra replied dully. "You want the hours too?"

"Seriously?"

"Yep. It's like being in prison. I'm counting the days until freedom." She met his eyes. "But I'll miss some parts."

"Me too." Elijah swallowed hard, averting his gaze, and focusing on the IV machine. It reminded him of seeing Graham in the hospital.

Working with her encouraged him to stop walking in Graham's shadow. She emboldened him. He had no right to feel anything for Tiandra beyond friendship. More than that, Tiandra valued him, developing his confidence and capability. She included him as though he was as much a part of this mission as she and the task force were. And for that, he was very grateful. Even if it meant hiding his own feelings and never telling Tiandra how deeply he'd fallen for her.

Tiandra slid into the passenger seat of the SUV. Bosco poked his head over the console and greeted her with lavishing kisses. She laughed, stroking his ears. "Hey, buddy. I missed you too." She hugged his neck, then twisted around, snapping her seat belt in place. Last, she donned her sunglasses to reduce the blinding afternoon light.

The sun transformed the snow-covered ground into a million shimmering diamonds.

"Ready?" Elijah slid behind the wheel.

"Beyond ready to wrap up this case."

"Can't wait to get away from me?" he teased.

If only he knew the truth. Tiandra studied Elijah.

Though he resembled Graham in so many ways, she noticed how Elijah's eyes seemed to smile with him, and his expressions were softer. Her mother said a person's personality painted them beyond their looks. She was right. Both Graham and Elijah were handsome, without a doubt. But the twins were individuals too. All that lingered between her and Graham didn't exist for her and Elijah. She'd made him bear burdens he didn't earn.

"Wow, take your time answering," Elijah joked, starting the engine.

Tiandra chuckled nervously. Did she dare confess her thoughts and feelings? "No, that's the only part that I'm not looking forward to."

He met her gaze, lingering a moment too long. "Me too." He pulled out of the hospital parking lot.

"I've enjoyed getting to know you," Tiandra confessed. "I always wondered how parents could tell their twins apart, but after spending time with you and Graham, I see the minor differences. And the major ones."

"Like what?"

Tiandra bit her lip. Why had she mentioned this? Now she'd be stuck providing more information. "Well, Graham's a little…rougher around the edges than you."

"Are you saying I'm a softie?" He chuckled. "I'm not sure how to take that."

"No, silly. He's just not as easy to talk to. You and I have a lot in common with our appreciation of the outdoors, Bosco, stuff like that." At the mention of his name, the K-9 appeared again between them and laid his head on the console.

Elijah stroked the canine. "Yeah. Bosco's amazing."

"Graham's never been really into him."

"That's part of our history. I told you our parents didn't allow pets. He's uncomfortable with them."

"The way your brother flirts with women, he doesn't seem uncomfortable around anyone."

Elijah snorted. "Yeah, that skill developed early and isn't one I possess."

She smiled, settling into the seat.

"I assume you were aware of his feelings for you?"

Tiandra did a double take. "Say what?"

"Or not." Elijah gripped the steering wheel. "Disregard. New topic."

"Negative. What're you saying?"

Elijah exhaled. "Graham talked about developing feelings for a coworker. You."

"Could've been Skyler."

"No, not the way he described the woman. It's you."

"Wait. Did he mention my name?"

"Not specifically, but he mentioned a coworker often."

Tiandra got quiet. Was that why Graham had gone to Walsh asking for her removal from the case? Because he cared for her? Was he protecting her? She groaned. "Wow, I might've totally mis-judged Graham."

"How so?"

"You're going to hate me when I tell you."

"Never. Try me."

Tiandra explained how Graham had wanted her taken off the Op, deeply wounding her. And that she'd considered his actions a backstabbing event.

Something flickered in Elijah's expression that she couldn't quite explain. "I understand why you'd go there."

"Thank you for saying that. I feel like a real jerk right now."

"Why? You didn't know."

"Yeah, but I jumped to conclusions, right into thinking bad things when I should've thought the best of him."

"You were partners. It's understandable you'd feel betrayed by his actions. Anybody would've re-acted the same." Elijah reached to touch her hand. "More importantly, now you see it through a differ-ent lens. When Graham recovers, you two should talk it over and work out the details."

"Yeah, we need to clear the air. Especially re-garding any romantic feelings."

Elijah withdrew his hand, his shoulders slumped. "I agree."

"I have to explain, kindly, that the emotion isn't mutual."

"What?" Was that relief she saw in Elijah's expression?

"No offense, but I don't view Graham that way. We're coworkers. Partners. Nothing more. He's just not my type."

"Oh." Elijah's reply was so soft she wasn't sure he'd actually said anything. "That'll be a new conversation for him. He's used to women swooning at his feet."

Tiandra chuckled. "Yeah, he's quite the flirt. You're not like that." She bit her lip, regretting letting the words escape.

"True. One of the many differences between Graham and I." Elijah's eyes remained on the road. "Most ladies prefer his approach."

"Oh, please, I'm sure you've had your fair share of swooning females." She playfully punched his arm.

Elijah snorted. "Not even close."

"Tell me."

"Later." He turned on the radio, filling the cab with joyous carols. "Hard to believe it's almost Christmas with all that's going on."

Disappointed by his shift in topics, Tiandra redirected the conversation. "Yeah, we don't get much time off to enjoy the holidays."

Clearly, she'd overstepped a boundary, and she'd not do it again. But being in Elijah's presence was tough and getting harder by the day. His alluring personality challenged her to become a better person. She loved his soft-spoken ways and kindness. She'd never met anyone like him, and he'd raised the bar for any man she'd meet in the future.

They entered a rural area as they headed for Mikko's home outside Deadwood. The task force cell phone rang, and Tiandra quickly answered. Elijah pulled to the side of the road behind a large Quonset building.

"Hey, guys," Skyler greeted.

"We're almost to Mikko's, so we'll have to turn off the cell after this," Tiandra said.

"Good, I caught you just in time then. The whole team's here. We got word back on Graham's evidence report."

"Oh?" Tiandra positioned the device between her and Elijah.

"Someone cut Graham's brakes, and we have a witness who places a black chromed-out Mercedes sedan at the scene."

"Like Mikko's car?" Tiandra clarified.

"Yes, ma'am."

"Did the witness identify Mikko as the driver?" Tiandra asked.

"No, the trucker said he couldn't see through the Mercedes tinted windows," Eliana said, joining the conversation.

"Mikko wouldn't hand over the keys to Penny," Elijah argued.

"It's possible someone else borrowed his car that night," Tiandra said.

"True." Elijah ran a hand over his head.

"Eliana got through Graham's old cell phone and found an out-of-focus picture of a woman meeting with Mikko," Skyler said. "The picture was taken from a reasonable distance. Doesn't give us much to zoom in on, however, the woman resembles Penny."

"She is Mikko's girlfriend," Tiandra said.

"Except the image doesn't look like a couple in love," Skyler added. "It's more of a business transaction."

"We're certain it's not Penny," Eliana said. "Her hair is shorter and she has tattoos on her left forearm."

"Penny doesn't have tattoos?" Elijah asked.

"Nope. She's allergic to the ink," Tiandra said.

"Wow, how'd I miss that?" Elijah mumbled.

"Graham claimed there was an insider." This time it was Chance who spoke. "You think it's Mikko or this mystery woman?"

"It's a definite possibility," Tiandra replied.

"One last thing," Eliana said, regaining everyone's attention. "Graham had typed in cryptic notes regarding the insider on his phone. Specifically noting both gangs."

"He thought the person worked for the 29 Locos and the Kings?" Tiandra asked.

"Yes, which provides free access to both," Eliana agreed. "We're still working on the numbers, although we've concluded the first is a date."

"03/01 and 01-838775," Walsh inserted.

"March 2001," Elijah recalled. "The second sounds like a case number."

"That's what we're thinking," Skyler added.

Tiandra tilted her head. "Maybe an old DEA investigation? Where did Graham work prior?"

"Saint Louis Police Department," Elijah offered.

Riker spoke next. "We're working on both agencies."

Tiandra smiled. "We're gaining ground."

"Yeah, the team's doing double time to get you guys out of there," Walsh said.

"Since Mikko's unaware of the deal date and location, be ready," Elijah said. "We'll receive the go command out of the blue."

"Roger that," Chance replied.

Elijah glanced at the time on the dashboard digital readout. "We need to get going. Mikko's got us on a short leash."

"Be safe, you guys. We're praying for you," Walsh assured, then hung up.

Elijah glanced over. "It's getting closer to the end. I can feel it."

Tiandra tucked the phone deep into her boot. "I hope you're right because if not, Mikko's got us right where he wants us. Without backup, no way to contact the team without him watching, and under his thumb."

TWELVE

Tiandra slipped into her boots, using the moonlight streaming through the blinds. With a single snap of her fingers, Bosco hurried to join her. "Ready?" she whispered, snapping on his leash.

Two thumps of his muscular tail said Bosco agreed.

They exited the bedroom, pausing to glimpse the nightstand clock. 05:00 glowed in blue LED numbers. She prayed Elijah waited for her on the porch as she gripped the knob and gently turned, tugging open the door.

She led the way, Bosco in perfect stride beside her, his nails clicking softly on the hardwood floor. A silent exit was impossible, but they did their best to quietly tread down the hallway. Loud snores emanated from Mikko's room. He'd stayed up late, indulging in substances that she hoped kept the man unconscious for a while. She and Elijah hadn't spoken privately since arriving at Mikko's house two nights before. Mikko seemed ever present and did not let up on his order prohibiting them from going anywhere without his permission.

The only exception to that ridiculous and overbearing rule was Tiandra taking Bosco outdoors for breaks. She'd sarcastically offered to wake him to join her, but after she'd interrupted him the first night he agreed to let her go outside alone. Without Bosco, she was certain Mikko would hold them prisoner in the house.

Tiandra glanced down at the Malinois, once more grateful for her K-9 partner and the minor reprieve.

They made their way to the steps and Tiandra recalled the photo of a young, clean-cut Mikko posing with two older men in front of a massive cornfield spanning into the distance that sat atop Mikko's nightstand. The single anomaly in his ju-venile-inspired decoration had captured Tiandra's attention the night before. She'd not had a chance to closely view the picture before he caught her and yelled for her to stay out of his room. She relied on her recollection of it, connecting the evidence dots from the case file.

Mikko was the son of a Nebraska farmer and he clearly held that memory dear. She needed to send a copy of the photo to the team via text, which was why she had to speak with Elijah. Without his help to occupy Mikko, she couldn't sneak into the man's bedroom. Whatever Mikko's reasons for keeping the picture close, sentimental or otherwise, she wanted HFTF to follow up on it. They already knew his father's land had exchanged hands sev-eral times and was currently owned by a large cor-poration, typical for farmland. However, Tiandra wondered if it had anything to do with the case and the upcoming drug deal. She'd leave no stone unturned in this Op.

She reached the front door and exhaled a breath, entering the security code. A peculiar precaution on Mikko's part, considering the alarm wouldn't notify the police. Instead, it would alert him and the Kings should someone enter or exit unauthorized. Again, Tiandra was grateful for Bosco and the need to go outside. It was the only place she and Elijah could speak freely, though they maintained precautions for bugs near the house.

The alarm light turned from red to green and the lock released. She tugged open the door and stepped out, inhaling deeply. The motion sensor triggered the porch light.

She made it to the edge of the steps when a beep sounded behind her.

Tiandra froze.

"Where do you think you're going?" Mikko demanded.

Tiandra forced herself not to startle. He enjoyed intimidation techniques, and she refused to give him the satisfaction. She twisted to face him, still gripping the leash. "Bosco needs a bathroom break." As though that wasn't perfectly obvious at five o'clock in the morning.

Mikko snorted. "Just make sure it's fast."

"Of course." Tiandra turned again, but was halted halfway by a beefy hand slamming down on her previously injured shoulder.

"I'm watching."

She gritted her teeth, forcing away the urge to thrust her elbow into his nose. "We'll be quick."

"Uh-huh." He laughed sardonically.

Bosco gave a low growl, and Mikko's expression darkened. He lifted the gun he always carried, aiming it at the dog.

Tiandra shifted, putting herself between the Malinois and weapon. "Bosco, down," she ordered, refraining from using the attack command.

Mikko shoved her hard, and Tiandra caught herself to prevent tripping down the steps.

In her periphery she spotted Mikko pinning her with another too long gaze before spinning on his heel and closing the door. He'd return to bed, but she needed to be careful.

She stepped onto the sidewalk, Bosco leading the way. Though Mikko's two-story home was decent—considering he was a drug dealer and bachelor—living under his control was suffocating. Worse than house arrest.

Tiandra considered all Elijah had shared with her about Mikko's ignorance of the drug deal details, indicating someone higher on the food chain called the shots. It seemed complications increased.

Bosco sniffed the extensive yard, where a six-foot privacy fence surrounded the property. The house sat in a rural area with no neighbors within a two-mile radius, providing Mikko the discretion for his nefarious comings and goings. And too far for her to run for help.

"Hey."

Tiandra spun, startled, and exhaled relief at Elijah's presence. How had she missed his approach?

"Slipped out before you," he replied to her unspoken question. "Did Mikko give you any trouble?"

"Nothing more than his usual intimidation games."

Elijah's eyes narrowed. "Did he hurt you?"

"No, but I can't tell you how much I'd love to see Bosco get the last word." She grinned in what she hoped was a reassuring manner.

"The day is coming." Elijah tucked his hands into his parka pockets.

The sun wouldn't rise for a while, leaving the atmosphere hovering in a hazy gray. The porch light cast a soft glow over the yard, fading near the fence, which provided shadows for them to linger in. Exactly where Tiandra preferred to be. Even if Mikko had bugs or cameras planted on the exterior of the house—which no doubt he did—the distance would ensure he couldn't eavesdrop, especially with her back turned and voice low.

"Have you been able to reach Penny?"

"No." She faced Elijah, whispering, "She's ghosted me."

"I've noticed she's not around much. That's strange."

"Have you asked Mikko about it?"

"Tried. He's not talking. Something's changed."

"Agreed." Tiandra shuffled closer to an evergreen tree near the fence. "I'm worried. Either she knows something and Mikko doesn't want her to share it or she's hurt. Maybe…" She gulped. "Worse."

"No way. Mikko wouldn't hurt her." Elijah's tone lacked conviction. "What about you? Did you get any sleep?"

She shrugged. "I'm getting used to the two or three hours a night. Keeps me on my toes." She offered him a sideways grin.

"Or you're delirious," he teased.

"That too. How about you?"

"Same." Elijah dug at the snow with his boot. "He's always watching."

"It's creepy." Tiandra scooted toward him, brushing her arm against his, and told him about the picture.

"Okay. I'll find a way to distract him so you can get into his room," he assured her.

"Thanks." She maintained the proximity to him.

Bosco investigated a small flowering bush covered by snow.

"If I lose Penny as a contact, I'm unsure where to start. Mikko's brought us into the fold and pushed others out. It doesn't give me a lot to work with," Tiandra confessed.

He glanced up at the sky. "I never realized how isolating this life was."

Tiandra understood he meant being undercover. "I'd like to say you get used to it, but that's not true."

"I usually have to work alone," he whispered. "It's nice to have someone to lean on." He gave her a gentle nudge with his shoulder. "I'm enjoying the company."

"Same." She smiled. "I need to get out of here to talk to Penny."

"Okay, let's work on that today."

"How?"

A slow grin crept across Elijah's face. "Leave that to me."

Elijah pulled up to the hideout. Convincing Mikko to let him and Tiandra leave was no simple task. He'd finally warned Mikko that danger wouldn't always come to them. They needed to be proactive. He used the excuse of checking out the hideout, alluding to issues there. For whatever reason, that worked, freeing them of the man's annoying presence.

"I'm impressed you pulled this off," Tiandra said.

Elijah shrugged. "I started worrying I wouldn't."

"What was the trick?"

"I made it his idea." Elijah chuckled. "He's such an egomaniac."

"Brilliant," Tiandra said. "What's Mikko believe we're doing?"

"He wants us to snoop and see if anyone is talking about the deal. He's heard rumblings that the 29 Locos are threatening a gang war within the next few days."

"That's new." She quirked a brow.

"Sure, after I told him there were."

"Gotcha." Tiandra chuckled. "Nobody will talk around us. I mean, they haven't up 'til now. I'd be shocked if they suddenly started."

"Shh, it took me forever to convince Mikko they would." Elijah gave her a playful nudge.

"My bad. Yes, of course they will divulge everything to us," Tiandra teased. "Roger that."

Lights glowed from every window and loud bass music pulsed from the inside the house. A few Kings meandered along the main floor, visible through the windows.

"Slim crew. So far, I've counted four guys and two women, but I don't recognize them," Elijah said.

"They're all low-level players or wannabes," Tiandra advised. "Hmm, must be a party or something elsewhere. The rest of the gang isn't here."

"Why didn't they invite us?" Elijah asked. "Is that concerning?"

"Not sure," Tiandra admitted. "Could mean we've been made or just that the news didn't travel.

Mikko had us under house arrest. It wasn't like we had much communication outside of him."

"True."

"But the advantage is there aren't many Kings here," she said, leaning forward in her seat to slide her Glock into her waistband. "Should be easy enough to get them talking to us. Prior to the accident, Graham and I hung with the Kings without issue. That took months to establish."

"Hopefully I don't undo all of it by saying the wrong thing."

"Less is more." She winked.

"Got it."

"Let's make sure we're scen and then find someplace to talk."

Elijah shut off the engine. "Works for me."

They slid from the vehicle, and he rounded the hood as Tiandra released Bosco, snapping on his leash. They approached the house and Elijah felt the eyes of the two men on the porch watching them with intensity and disdain. The hate was palpable, and he had the urge to pull his gun from his waistband. But drawing it would only create an aura of defensiveness and draw unwanted attention.

They moved up the walkway, Elijah leading.

"Hey, G," the younger of the two said.

In a single moment of panic, he wondered if he needed to call thc guy by name, then chose arrogance instead. He lifted his chin in a quick jerk of acknowledgment.

The other man turned his back and brushed past him, colliding shoulders in an aggressive act before walking away without a word.

"Just ignore him," Tiandra whispered. "Haters gonna hate."

Though she played off the behavior, after hearing what she'd said about the relationships she and Graham had worked to establish, he recognized worry in her expression.

They entered the hideout and moved into the living room, then aimed for the kitchen, where the others loitered. He didn't engage with them. Instead, he hovered near Tiandra, listening.

She offered a glance over her shoulder before stepping away from him, maintaining earshot distance. Tiandra approached two women leaning against the dining room wall, speaking in low tones. Elijah shifted, one eye on Tiandra, the other surveying the area.

"Hey. Where's Penny?" Tiandra asked.

With a condescending once-over, the first woman shook her head.

The other glared at Tiandra. "Do I look like her mama? How should I know?" She stormed out of the room.

The first woman appeared lost. "You Mikko's number two now?"

"G is." Tiandra shrugged with a bored reply and rolled her eyes. That earned her a grunt before she walked away to join her friend.

"That was fun," Tiandra mumbled, returning to stand by Elijah.

They moved to the dining room and sat at the table. The men in the kitchen exited the space without a backward glance.

The house had cleared out. "Was it something I said?" Elijah asked, sarcasm thick.

"No, you just took a position they don't think you deserve," a woman replied from behind them.

He'd not seen her before. Had she come through the back door? She wore jeans, boots, and a black hoodie pulled up over her head. Except for a few stray blonde strands, the fabric concealed her hair. He glanced at Tiandra. Did she recognize the newcomer?

Tiandra sat back in her seat, assuming a disinterested position, Bosco taking his place beside her. "We're on the outs?"

"Beats me." The woman shrugged. "Just saying. You gotta prove you deserve to be here."

"Doesn't Mikko determine that?" Elijah asked.

"Guess you'd better ask him. But you jumping to the top of the pile means you stepped on someone else's toes. That didn't earn you friends." She left, following the others.

"At least we know why we're not welcome here." Elijah slumped in his seat.

Engines started and faded, confirming the Kings weren't interested in hanging out with them.

"Now what?" Tiandra groaned.

"We enjoy our freedom?" Elijah chuckled.

"Let's look around." Tiandra pushed away from the table, and they meandered through the house. They passed an obviously poorly hidden camera, and she rolled her eyes.

The Kings had wrecked the home, as usual. Trash littered every conceivable place. Old food rotted on the kitchen counters and coffee table. They'd stripped the beds, leaving sheets and blankets lying on the floor. The environment screamed squatter or rave party.

"And I didn't think it would get worse from when I was rooming here," he said.

"When the deal is done, they'll move to a new location. Hopefully, Mikko allows us to stay with him," she said, a little louder than necessary. No doubt for Mikko's prying ears and benefit.

"How can we earn the Kings' trust?" Elijah played along.

"Prove our loyalty. Show them we're cool so they understand we're protecting Mikko," Tiandra replied with enthusiasm. "Whatever it takes, right?"

"Right," Elijah agreed.

They cleared the house, locating only trash.

"Best return to Mikko's. Nothing here for him to worry about," he said loudly. "He'll be disappointed."

"Yeah." Tiandra sighed.

The sound of screeching tires filled the atmosphere. Elijah and Tiandra rushed to the window.

Two vehicles had pulled up to the front of the house. Instinct warned Elijah they needed to leave.

They started for the stairs, but the rush of footsteps below halted them in place.

"Knock, knock," a man's voice taunted.

Elijah and Tiandra exchanged a look and spun on their heels. Just in time. Automatic rounds ricocheted everywhere, piercing the drywall and floorboards beneath them. They had to take cover. Elijah gripped Tiandra's hand and pulled her toward the bedroom at the far end of the hall where he'd stayed.

"Get the dresser and mattresses," he whispered.

They dragged the objects to barricade the door and buy time. He ripped off the remaining flat sheet and handed it to Tiandra.

"Hold on to this."

Gunfire continued below them, moving upstairs.

Tiandra hurried to the window, then turned to face him. "It's bolted shut! We're trapped!"

"No, we're not!" Elijah tugged open the closet doors and pointed upward. "There's an attic entrance in here."

Tiandra joined him in pulling down the door with the half ladder. Elijah helped Tiandra up, then together they hoisted Bosco through the opening.

Loud thumps against the outer door conveyed their pursuers were determined to break through.

"Come on!" she urged, her arms reaching for him.

"Not yet!"

"What?"

Elijah rushed from the closet and grabbed an old boot and blanket tossed haphazardly on the floor. He wrapped his arm in the blanket, and using the boot, shattered the window. The cold winter night air blew through. Next, he destroyed the overhead light, plunging the space into darkness.

The pounding grew louder, and the wood door frame splintered.

Elijah rushed to the closet, closing the door behind him, and secured it by wrapping his belt tightly around the clothes rod.

"Hurry," Tiandra whispered.

He spun, gripping the ladder to hoist himself up, and joined Tiandra and Bosco.

Together they tugged closed the attic door and waited.

THIRTEEN

Tiandra's heart drummed against her ribs so hard she feared breaking one. She hoped Elijah's ruse would work, convincing the intruders they'd escaped out the window once they breached the door.

Please let them go away. The fervent prayer floated from Tiandra even as her teeth chattered with panic.

The sound of the shooters below was too close. They carried extensive firepower that she and Elijah had no expectation of countering with their pistols. She whispered, "Shh," to Bosco.

The Malinois's soft pants conveyed he too understood the urgency of the moment.

Tiandra and Elijah remained stone-still, visually surveying the space in the dark. The attic spanned the entire length of the house. Pink insulation overhead and sections of drywall covered one side, evidence someone had started remodeling it. Three windows overlooked the property facing west, north, and south.

Though she longed to get a better view of it all, she dared not move or risk using her cell phone to illuminate the space.

She and Elijah relied on touch and the moonlight glowing through the windows. One of the windows would be their means of escape.

Elijah pointed to the bedsheet she still held in her hand. "Rip it into long strips and we'll tie them together," he whispered.

In cooperation, they made short work of the task, careful to minimize the sound as much as possible.

The thudding below said the men were actively trying to break through the door.

She and Elijah got on their knees and crept to the largest of the three windows with already broken sharp edges that provided the start they needed. Elijah used a piece of wood left from a dollhouse stored in the attic to finish breaking out the rest of the glass.

"It's going to be a tight fit," he warned. "I'm not sure I can make it. But you and Bosco will. Get out of here and distract them. I'll go back down the ladder."

"No way," she argued. "I'm not leaving you behind."

"We don't have any other options."

Tiandra inched closer to the window, glancing out. No one appeared.

The men's voices carried to them, indicating they'd entered the bedroom. Within seconds, if Elijah's trick didn't work, they'd find the closed closet door and barrel through it too.

"They're looking for us," she whispered.

Elijah grunted. "Yep, and if they believe the ruse, assuming we escaped out the north-facing bedroom window, it buys us time. They won't spot us climbing out the south side window."

Just as he said it, the footsteps faded. The men exited the house through the back door. She peered from the corner of the window. Her gaze landed on the automatic weapons they carried.

"They're leaving," Tiandra said incredulously. "That's strange. Is it me, or was that too easy?"

"Yeah, they're not going. Not yet."

Bosco shifted, whining.

Movement in the shadows outside caught Tiandra's gaze. She spotted a man hauling a gas can. "He's starting a fire!"

"We have to get out of here."

Elijah finished tying the sheet and seemed to study the window.

Tiandra watched as the man with the gas can bolted out of sight around the house toward the front door. No doubt intending to ignite the flames there, and flush Tiandra and Elijah out the back door, where they waited to shoot them.

Elijah anchored the other end of the sheet rope to one of the floor joists. Tiandra prayed it held.

"Ready?"

She nodded and lifted Bosco into her arms. Elijah wrapped the fabric around them, securing it, and she climbed out of the window with Bosco, steadily rappelling down the side of the house. Her boots bounced against the wood siding, making more noise than she wanted. Shouting from the opposite end of the house sent her pulse racing.

Almost at the bottom.

And then she smelled the gasoline.

The house was on fire.

She glanced up and caught Elijah gazing down at her, holding tight to the sheet to ensure she made it safely.

Tiandra finished the descent, unraveling herself and Bosco from the fabric, then gestured for Elijah to follow.

He ducked through the window, disappearing from sight, no doubt double checking the sheet's attachment to the floor joist. Then Elijah returned, placing a leg over the ledge and prepared to descend.

Flames exploded around them.

Bosco jerked toward the front of the house.

Tiandra fought to keep him quiet as she silently urged Elijah to hurry.

He slid down the sheet in record time, releasing his hold with the remaining four feet below him, landing with a hard thud next to her.

They sprinted into the tree line away from the inferno consuming the house.

Fire decimated the hideout. Neither stopped running until they'd reached a considerable distance. Panting from the cold and exertion, they paused behind a decrepit shed and surveyed the flames high into the sky.

"Those weren't Kings," Tiandra said.

"Nope. I'm guessing 29 Locos Cartel."

Tiandra dropped onto an old barrel. Beside her, Bosco panted, his breaths making puffy clouds in the night air. "Did the low-level players who left earlier contact them?"

"Or were they waiting for us?" Elijah extended a hand to her, helping Tiandra to her feet. "We need to keep going."

They walked at a normal pace, both huffing after the exciting escape.

"We can't walk back to Mikko's," she said.

"Agreed."

They crested a hill, spotting a structure in the valley. "There."

"Good eyes!"

The trek down the hill wasn't easy with the snowy ground and slippery patches of ice. When they finally reached the bottom, they walked to the edge of what Tiandra recognized as an old, abandoned barn.

"Do we tell Mikko?" Elijah asked.

"Why wouldn't we?"

He shrugged. "It seems to me that things are getting a little too convenient. Like Mikko arguing about us coming here and then the Kings shrug us off as if we're enemy number one, only to have the 29 Locos Cartel burst in to eliminate us."

"Definitely no coincidence."

"Why would Mikko pull us into the fold and then try to get rid of us?" Elijah moved further into the barn. "There's a lot of hay in here."

Tiandra joined him. "They must use this as an overage shelter or something."

Together they settled inside where the prickly straw was fullest. "It's warmer than it is outside," Elijah said.

"Is it bad I'd rather stay out here than go back to Mikko's?" Tiandra asked.

"Nope." Elijah settled into a pooled bale of straw. "It's actually kinda cozy."

"How long do we hide out here?" Tiandra asked.

"At least until the 29 Locos Cartel believes they won. Our Glocks are no match against their firepower." Elijah folded his hands, sitting forward so his elbows rested on his knees. "Get comfortable." He patted the space beside him, and Bosco joined him.

Tiandra chuckled. "You've made a lifetime friend."

Elijah petted the Malinois. "I can live with that." He glanced up at her.

The moonlight shone through the barn's broken frame, giving them ambient light. In another setting, it might've been romantic. Tiandra shoved that unwanted thought aside. "What canine breed will you want to start with when you return to Sioux City?" she asked, diverting the conversation to remind her of the temporary situation with Elijah.

"Any. I always wanted a dog." He continued petting Bosco, then tilted his head, studying her.

"Why are you looking at me like that?"

"I'm picturing you as a nurse."

She dropped beside him. "That seems like a lifetime ago." She'd already told him about her father's murder. She'd not rehash those painful memories again.

"Tell me about your siblings."

Tiandra groaned.

"Aw, c'mon. We're killing time here."

She sighed. "After Daddy's death, we got closer. Closed ranks and all that. But then Anissa went off the deep end. My oldest sister, Meghan, demanded I fix the problem since I was closest to Anissa." Tiandra used a piece of straw to draw circles in the dirt floor.

"That's kind of unfair. Why you?"

"Anissa listened to me. She was always the wild child. I loved her spirit, though. Fun and brave. She was outgoing and courageous. She's the one who encouraged me to join the FBI."

"Sounds pretty amazing."

"Yeah." Memories of Anissa tackled her heart. "We never really knew what happened. One day Anissa was her usual energetic self, the next, she's drug addicted. How did we miss that?"

Elijah remained quiet, and she appreciated that he didn't try to provide platitudes to help her feel better.

"Anyway, Anissa's overdose was like someone cutting the thread holding us together. The family parted ways, and we started unraveling." The reminder of Meghan's last message had Tiandra pausing. "Then right before I had the car crash, Meghan tried contacting me. I never responded."

"There's still time." Elijah placed his hand over hers.

"I'm calling her as soon as this is over."

"I understand." Elijah shook his head. "I'm sorry for getting all personal on you."

Strangely, she wanted to tell him about her life. To share that part of her history with someone. And she longed to know more about him. "I don't mind. It's just with my job, I have to hide a lot from my family. I can't exactly tell them about our undercover Ops and stuff. That annoys them."

"But it's for their protection as much as yours," Elijah said.

"Yeah, but they don't share that view. When Anissa first got involved with drugs, they looked to me as the fixer. I tried, I really did. But she was in deep, and it was like I was fighting an invisible force field that kept drawing her back. When she finally got the bad stuff, the one that killed her, they blamed me."

"What? That's so wrong!" Elijah blurted. "Sorry."

"That's normal, though, with grieving. People want someone to blame. Meghan said with my job and connections, I should've stopped her and the dealers. She's right. It's on me."

"No single person can fight against addiction. That must come first from the one who is addicted," Elijah said. "And please, trying to stop all the drugs? How long has law enforcement worked toward that goal?"

Tiandra hung her head. Her eyes stung. "True." Secretly, she agreed with her family. "I was always her protector. Fighting off the bullies, fixing her boo-boos with Band-Aids and kisses. I just lost the battle with the worst bully of all." No longer able to contain the threatening tears, Tiandra allowed herself to cry.

Before she knew it, Elijah had pulled her into an embrace, and she let him. Tired of being strong, she needed a few minutes to feel the pain that she pretended wasn't there for the sake of holding herself together.

His touch was tough, enveloping, and warm.

For the first time in her life since her father had died, Tiandra's self-preservation melted, allowing her to enter a safe place where she could grieve her most painful losses.

Holding Tiandra felt natural, and yet, Elijah's heart ached. His awkwardness with women had plagued him since childhood. He wondered what Graham would do in this situation.

"Thank you." Tiandra withdrew, wiping at her face with her sleeve.

"Are you okay?"

She nodded. "I've needed to do that for years."

"Glad I could help," he replied, searching his coat pockets. "Sorry, I don't have a tissue."

Tiandra chuckled, pulling a tissue from her jacket pocket. "I always have one handy." She groaned. "I'm slowly becoming my mother."

Elijah laughed. "She raised a wonderful woman, so I'd say that's probably not a bad thing."

She lowered her hand, tilting her head, and soaked him in her hazel eyes. Though he couldn't see her clearly in the darkened barn, he'd memorized the color, recalling it easily as she sat beside him.

"No more talk about me." Tiandra settled into the hay and tugged Bosco closer, creating a barrier between them. Elijah took the hint and scooted back in his place. "Your turn."

"Um, maybe I should check and see if they've gone." Elijah got to his feet and scurried from the barn, glancing toward the hideout. Orange and yellow flames still stretched into the sky. "We could call Mikko and get a ride out of here."

"Not yet," Tiandra said as he returned to where she sat. "Talk to me."

Elijah groaned and dropped onto a bale of hay. "Fine. What do you want to know?"

"What's the deal with you and Graham?"

He quirked a brow. "What do you mean?"

"Neither of you says much about the other. I figured you'd regale me with tales from your childhood, but you rarely talk about him. He's the same way."

"We used to be close." Elijah picked at a section

of the straw, unsure where to start. "That changed after high school."

"Why?"

She'd confessed truths to him, earning the right to some of his secrets.

"When we were in college, before I went to the academy, I was in a serious relationship with a girl named Nell. Thought we'd get married, have kids, the whole picture." Thoughts he'd buried of Nell bounced to the forefront of his mind.

"What happened?"

"Graham."

Tiandra gasped. "He hit on her?"

"No." Elijah shook his head. "Honestly, it wasn't his fault, but I blamed him. Right before I proposed to Nell, I overheard her talking on the phone to her best friend. She confessed she was in love with Graham and had hoped she'd get closer to him by using me."

"Oh, Elijah." Tiandra put a hand over her mouth. "I'm so sorry. How awful."

"Yeah."

"Did Graham find out?"

"Yes, and he wasn't interested in her at all. He thought she was disgusting for doing that to me, but it still dug deep."

"I can't imagine."

"Talk about a betrayal." He sighed. "But life was always like that. Me competing with Graham. Whatever I did, he did it better. He shines everywhere he goes. My parents used to say, 'You should be more like Graham.'"

"Ouch, that's harsh," Tiandra said.

Elijah shrugged. "They meant it as a compliment to him, but I don't know if they really understood how their words hurt me. The thing was, I wanted to imitate Graham. He could talk to anyone in his smooth manner. Always made friends easier, was stronger, superior at everything. If I didn't resent him so much, I'd admire him." He choked back a bitter laugh.

"I understand why you'd feel that way, but I think you're pretty amazing."

"You do?" The question sounded childish and insecure. For the first time, not being compared to Graham—at least not in a manner that elevated him over Elijah—enraptured him.

"Um, yeah." Tiandra twisted toward him, moving Bosco who rose and sniffed near the door. They sat knee to knee, facing one another. "You have a great sense of humor. You're humble, not overbearing. And you're great with dogs. Even Bosco likes you."

At the mention of his name, the Malinois trotted to them.

Elijah smiled.

"I figure if he approves, then I can trust you," Tiandra said. "Bosco's picky."

Elijah bent forward, inhaling Tiandra's sweet scent. He reached to touch her hand, allowing the

softness of her skin to linger beneath his fingertips. Moonlight cast a soft glow over her face. He
gently caressed her cheek. She closed her eyes and
Elijah moved closer.

Her breath warmed his nose.

She lifted her chin, and he leaned in for the kiss
he'd yearned for.

Elijah's cell phone rang and he jerked back. Tiandra sat up straighter. Withdrawing the device,
he glanced at the screen, though he already knew
the caller. "It's Mikko."

"Better answer it," she said.

Elijah's heart drummed so hard he could barely
hear over the pulse in his ears. What had he just
done? He had no right. Graham was in love with
Tiandra and regardless of whether she shared those
feelings, he had to honor his brother. The line rang
a second time. Elijah sucked in a breath, trying
to calm himself and handle the conversation with
Mikko. "Hello."

"Where are you?" Mikko barked.

"Funny you should ask. We got run out of the
hideout."

"By who?"

"That's what I'd love to know."

"They're watching." Mikko cursed. "29 Locos
is surveilling the Kings."

"They torched the hideout."

Mikko cursed again.

Bosco rose, nose to the ground, sniffing toward

the barn door. Elijah watched as Tiandra followed the dog outside. "We're staying low."

"Good idea."

"Any response from Penny?" Elijah asked.

"I'll be in touch." Mikko ignored him and disconnected.

Elijah got to his feet and trailed Tiandra. Near the entrance he spotted a piece of yellowed paper wedged between the dirt and a bale. He knelt, tugging the paper free. He lifted his cell phone and illuminated it. Only a portion of the original document remained, leaving partial information where weights and dates were listed on one side and the letters *okston* across the top.

"G!" Urgency in Tiandra's cry, and the use of his undercover name had Elijah jumping to his feet.

He tucked the paper into his pocket and rushed outside. "Where are you?"

"Here!" Her voice carried from the corner of the barn.

Jogging around the building, he spotted Bosco standing beside a large bale of hay. Tiandra knelt on the other side of it. "We need to call for help. Penny's hurt."

Elijah hurried to get a closer look. Penny lay wrapped in a blanket, with only her head peering from beneath it. Bruises covered her face in various shades, testifying to a severe beating.

"Hurry! Her breathing is shallow."

Elijah withdrew his phone and called 9-1-1.

"Nine-one-one. What's your emergency?"

"I need ambulance transport immediately. The victim is a young woman, probably late twenties or early thirties with multiple bruises and lacerations about the face. She's wrapped in a blanket. I don't want to risk removing it and endangering her to hypothermia."

Tiandra's eyes widened, and she ran her hand below her neck in a cutting motion and shook her head. What was wrong with her?

"Where is she located?" the operator asked.

"South of the junction of Highway 83 near County Road 44, about two miles east on the south side of the road. Labored breathing, serious condition."

"Sir, what's your name?"

Like an electric shock jolting him to the present, that single question made Elijah realize his mistake. "Please hurry." He disconnected.

"We have to go," Tiandra said.

Elijah opened his mouth, and she shook her head, placing a finger to her lips.

They tucked the blanket tighter around Penny to keep her warm, then he followed Tiandra away. With a visual of the road, they shifted to the side.

"You spoke like law enforcement," Tiandra said.

"I reverted." Elijah fisted his hands in frustration. "Old habits."

"We have to go now."

He knew that. Cops would accompany the ambulance, and they'd ask questions.

"We need to find who did this and we can't do that from inside an interrogation room," Tiandra whispered. "They'll take us in for questioning."

"We did nothing wrong," Elijah argued. "We can't leave her out here alone."

"Look at us."

Elijah surveyed Tiandra with her real-looking rub-on tattoos, motorcycle boots, jeans, and leather coat. Then he glanced down at his own arms and put a hand to his throat where the dragon tattoo remained. "They'll ask if we're part of the Kings."

"Right. And when we say yes, they'll take us in," Tiandra agreed. "Let's get to higher ground and watch. When we see Penny's taken care of, we'll head out."

Tiandra returned to where Penny lay and leaned down, her ear hovering above Penny's mouth. "Her breaths are labored. Someone beat her and left her for dead."

"If we hadn't found her, she would've died." Elijah scanned the distance. "Is someone watching us now? Are we still in danger?"

"I doubt it. They didn't hang around to confirm she'd died." Tiandra glanced down at her friend. "Besides, they had no way of knowing we'd run here." She leaned forward, gently brushing Penny's blood-matted hair away from her face. "Now I know why she hasn't been answering me."

"And Mikko's lack of concern for her has me wondering," Elijah whispered, using the phone light to examine Penny's many wounds. He winced. "Wow."

Tiandra nodded. "Definitely a rage beating."

Sirens wailed in the distance.

"Hold on, Penny. Help is coming," Tiandra cooed, stroking the woman's hair.

Strobing blue and red lights approached on the road.

Penny groaned, mumbling something unintelligible. They both froze, watching, listening. But she passed out again without another sound.

"Let's go."

Tiandra gave a sad nod. She lifted Bosco's leash. "But we stay near. I want to make sure she's cared for."

They shifted away from the scene into the field, hiding behind several boulders and trees where they watched as the ambulance pulled in. The medics rushed toward the barn, hollering orders at one another.

Elijah touched her arm, and they hurried into the tree line and disappeared in the foliage. Once they'd put enough distance between themselves and Penny, Tiandra contacted the task force, placing the call on speakerphone.

"We have to talk to Penny," Tiandra said. "Find out who did this."

"But we'll need to be careful about walking into the hospital," Elijah added.

"Agreed," Walsh said.

"Your enemy is growing bolder," Riker assessed.

"We'll meet you at the abandoned Halley farm off Route 86," Skyler said.

"Where are you now?" Walsh asked.

"Two miles east of the hideout," Elijah replied.

"Okay. There will be a green pickup on the next block, keys in the console," Skyler said, ending the call.

They walked to the hideout, cautiously approaching. They smelled it before they saw the damage.

The place had been burned beyond repair and the SUV Mikko had given them had suffered the same fate.

"Do we notify Mikko?" Tiandra asked.

"Not until we talk to Penny. He might've been her assailant." Elijah remembered the paper tucked into his pocket and passed it to her. "Hey, I found this inside the barn."

"What is it?"

"I'm not sure, but there's something familiar about it."

"You think it's a clue?"

"Yeah." Elijah studied the partial document. "But to what?"

FOURTEEN

As Skyler promised, the green pickup sat waiting for Tiandra and Elijah. A duffel bag filled with clothes rested on the floorboard.

Tiandra loaded Bosco on the bench seat between them, and slid behind the wheel, Elijah settled in the passenger scat. She drove until they'd reached a decrepit gas station off the side of a rural road.

"I'll change first," Tiandra said. "Watch Bosco and ensure they didn't follow us."

"Roger that," Elijah replied.

She got out of the truck, carrying the duffel. The attendant ignored her, intent on watching TV. Tiandra hurried to the restroom at the back of the store and quickly changed into the slacks, blouse, and heels provided inside. She refrained from donning the white doctor's jacket, deciding to wait until she got to the hospital. Skyler had included a brush and hair tie with a blonde wig and oversize glasses. Tiandra ran the bristles through her tangled hair and whipped it into a bun to hide it under the hairpiece later. She stuffed her dirty clothes into the bag, careful not to mess up the wig or jacket, and left it inside the stall, before returning to where Elijah sat waiting.

"Any issues?" She entered the truck.

"Nope, not a customer besides us, and the attendant never even looked up when you entered or exited. Must be an interesting show he's watching."

"I left the duffel bag on the toilet tank for you."

"Roger that." Elijah got out of the truck and closed the door. He disappeared through the gas station doors.

Tiandra didn't miss the dejection weighing on his shoulders. She wanted to comfort him but couldn't. His mistake in talking with the dispatcher, regardless of reasoning, could've cost them big time if Penny recalled the conversation.

Muscle memory was a real thing, and Elijah had reverted to his training under duress, speaking like a cop. Normally, that was a positive. This night, it posed a problem. Tiandra consoled herself with the reminder that Penny had only stirred briefly. For the most part, she'd been out of it. At least, Tiandra hoped so.

Elijah returned wearing the blue scrubs Skyler had provided. Taking Tiandra's lead, he'd not donned the wig, but he wore the glasses. Tiandra grinned. The round frames changed his appearance without detracting from his attractiveness. She gave herself a mental slap upside the head. *Knock it off.* His scrubs peeked out from under his unbuttoned winter coat as he climbed into the passenger seat wordlessly.

"I forgot to mention not to put the wig on yet," Tiandra said.

"I picked up on your cue. Besides, the attendant

said 'hello' when I walked in. Didn't want him to see the transformation."

"Good."

They drove quietly, both lost in their own thoughts. Walsh provided the hospital name where the medics had transported Penny along with her room number via text. Talking with her before anyone, especially Mikko arrived, was imperative. Tiandra ran through the plan with Elijah. He nodded, offering no input.

"We'll separate once we're inside," Tiandra said. "You guard the door while I talk to Penny. Warn me if we need to go."

"What's the signal?" Elijah asked.

"How about two quick raps on the door?"

"Works for me."

She entered the parking lot and aimed for the far side, where she spotted the orange electric car Skyler had said she'd driven. Tiandra parked next to it.

"Do not look at Skyler. Leave your door unlocked," she reminded him. "She'll take Bosco to the burger place off the highway, where we'll pick him up." Though they'd already gone over the plan several times, Tiandra reiterated everything to him.

To his credit, Elijah didn't argue or throw attitude. Another difference between him and Graham. He'd have fought her at every interaction.

"Questions?" She slid her arms into the white hospital coat and pulled on her wig. Elijah did the same, transforming his hair into short waves.

"Does it look okay?" he asked, pulling down the visor and adjusting the fit.

"Yes." She glanced down, grinning, and tugged the fake ID from inside the bag, attaching it to her outer pocket.

"You look good as a blonde," he said with a wink.

Tiandra twirled a tendril. "I might dye my hair after this mission."

He chuckled.

Grateful they were talking again, she smiled at him. He'd grown so quiet she'd worried whether he wanted to continue working with her. "Also, walk in like you own the place to avoid anyone asking if they can help us."

"Got it."

"Bosco, you go with Skyler, and I'll see you soon." She hugged him, then shut off the engine, avoiding eye contact with her teammate while exiting the truck.

She and Elijah strode toward the hospital and entered through the staff entrance on the side of the building, using the badge Skyler had provided. They walked through the brightly lit hallway. It was late, and the night shift was quieter and easier to maneuver around than the busy day personnel. Tiandra glimpsed her and Elijah's reflections in the decorative mirrors. Neither looked like themselves or their Kings' aliases. Perfect.

They rode to the fifth floor and exited the elevator, swiftly making their way through the dimly lit hall to Penny's room. Patients had settled in for the night, leaving the unit quiet.

"Go in and I'll keep watch," Elijah whispered, taking his place beside the door.

Visiting hospitals was becoming a little too common for Tiandra, and she hated it. She glanced to the right and left, the hairs on her neck rising though she didn't see danger. Women's voices at the far end of the hall had her pausing. Elijah waved and she ducked into Penny's room.

Soft light glowed over the hospital bed where Penny lay, eyes closed. Whooshing sounds and beeping from the machines played a strange symphony. Tiandra approached cautiously.

Her heart hitched at the sight of her friend. The medical staff had cleaned her face, though it still bore evidence of her horrific beating. Her bruised lip was split, and one eye had swollen completely shut. Both her cheeks were discolored in varying shades of blue and green.

"Hey, Penny," Tiandra said softly. "It's Tia."

She didn't open her eyes as she slurred a single word, "Loveprotesss."

"Who did this to you?"

"Mmm…" Penny's voice trailed off.

"Mikko?" Tiandra asked. Then silenced herself. She would not lead Penny to the answers she wanted to hear.

Penny rolled her head side to side, refuting the comment.

Tiandra rubbed her friend's hand. "Who hurt you?"

"Grr," Penny said.

Tiandra's full attention rested on the injured woman. Was she trying to say G? No way. Elijah had been with her the entire time.

"They talk," Penny mumbled.

"Who?" Tiandra's pulse ratcheted up a notch.

"Mikko promise grr," Penny slurred.

Graham? Did she know Graham's real identity, or did she mean Gray, the long version of Elijah's undercover name? "G?"

Penny moved slightly, leaving Tiandra unsure she'd actually nodded. "What promise?"

"Secrets." Her voice increased and decreased in octaves around the word. "Mikko knows."

Tiandra leaned closer. "What does he know?"

"It's coming out." Penny exhaled the last words. "Grr…" The word ended in a gurgling.

A click behind Tiandra froze her in place. A shift in the reflection on the IV machine had her whirling around and colliding hard with an object. Pain erupted behind her eyes, and a flash of light blinded her.

Someone swept her feet out from under her, and Tiandra flailed, striking her face against the hospital bed rail before crashing to the floor. In a whoosh, all the air fled from her lungs. Her attacker landed a blow to the back of her head and pounced, holding her down with a knee in her kidneys that pierced her body with immobilizing pain.

Emergency ringing outside the door drifted into the room.

Tiandra recalled the sound from her nursing days. Code Blue.

She fought, struggling to force the person off her or to scream, but failed to do either. Her attacker kept her face planted tight against the cold linoleum floor. From that position she spotted the remote dangling from the side of the bed. She needed to grab the emergency call button!

With all her strength, she reached for the device.

Tiandra could barely breathe past the pain in her kidneys, and the pressure against her back kept her from inhaling deeply. She tried again to grasp the remote, but a hand gripped her arm, the same arm that had been injured in the car accident, and twisted it backward. Tiandra yelped in agony.

The person moved, but before Tiandra processed the freedom, a kick to her ribs sent her sprawling. With one last effort, she reached, determined to grip the person's leg.

She tried to call for help but the words never left her lips.

A strike to the side of her neck plunged Tiandra into darkness.

Staff rushed through the hallway, responding to the loud emergency tone that emitted from a room around the corner.

Elijah paced near Penny's door, keeping out of

sight as much as possible. Though a nearby janitorial closet provided him a perfect hiding place, he had to maintain visual for Tiandra's protection.

Minutes later, a second call came over the speakers, this time rousing every medical professional into the hallway adjacent to him. He stepped to the side, avoiding eye contact as they passed.

None commented at him as they ran toward the blinking light above the second patient's room at the far end, where another nurse pushed a large cardio cart.

Two calls in one night, minutes apart. Was that normal?

Instinct had Elijah surveying the staff, shifting slightly from Penny's door.

"Hey, we need all hands on deck," a nurse said from behind him, grabbing his arm and dragging him with her.

"Coming," Elijah said, determined to break free but unsure how to do so without causing suspicion.

"Lee, here!" another nurse called, and the woman released her grip on Elijah.

He rushed to Penny's room. A different medical professional approached, and he ducked into a patient's doorway. When the hallway was clear, he turned and spotted Penny's open door.

He left his hiding place as a doctor walked by, making eye contact.

Elijah's heart plunged into a triple beat. His pulse raced.

Trapped.

But the man glanced down at his cell phone and headed toward the chiming Code Blue call.

Elijah rushed forward, seeing a woman resembling Tiandra exit Penny's room. He did a double take, his mind recalling Tiandra had worn a disguise—including a blond wig. The person sprinted away from him.

He gave chase, instincts blaring on high alert. She ducked into the stairwell ahead of him, slamming shut the door just as Elijah reached for the handle. He whipped it open, the sound of footfalls echoing below him.

He increased his pace, but quickly lost sight of the woman. A door slammed, reverberating in the stairwell. On which floor had she exited?

Elijah quickened his steps, determined to catch up, but when he got to the next door, it was locked. He continued his descent, intending to cut off the person, but when he bolted through the stairwell door, there was no sign of her.

He turned and slammed his hand on the door, then taking the stairs three and four at a time, he rushed to Penny's room.

The personnel were occupied with the two code-blue calls in the opposing patient rooms. With an exhaled relief, Elijah approached Penny's door just as it flew open, and a nurse sprinted out. Elijah ducked into the alcove until she passed him, exclaiming, "I need a doctor!"

Elijah bolted into Penny's room and spotted Tiandra pushing herself upright on the floor. He hoisted her into his arms and ran to the stairwell before the nurse returned.

"Wait, wait," Tiandra said.

He paused, and they watched through the small window in the steel door. Nurses and doctors entered Penny's room, and one rolled in a crash cart.

"What happened to her?" Tiandra asked.

"Should we go back?"

"No. We need to get out of here and notify the team."

He helped her to stand and through slower movements, they descended the stairs. She clung to the railing, refusing to let him carry her. At last, they reached the main floor and exited to the lobby and out the doors.

When they were outside, Elijah asked, "What happened?"

She pressed a hand to her neck. "Someone attacked me inside Penny's room."

"How? I was watching…" The words died on his lips. He'd been dragged from his post, leaving Tiandra exposed. He averted his eyes.

"He must've already been inside."

"It was a man?"

"No. Yes. I don't know."

"I saw a woman who resembled you—I mean like your normal self—come sprinting out of the room. I chased her but she eluded me."

They reached the pickup and Elijah helped Tiandra into the passenger seat before taking his place behind the steering wheel.

He wasted no time starting the engine and heading for the road.

Tiandra related the details of what occurred in Penny's room. "She never used Graham's name, but she kept saying 'grr'…"

"Like a growl?" Elijah asked.

"More like 'Graham,' but she never said the whole word."

"That's strange."

"No, something's different." Tiandra tugged off the wig. "She also said 'love protects.' Or at least that's what I think she meant. She was drugged and slurring her words. She passed out in the middle of 'grr,' and that's when the attacker hit me from behind."

Tiandra withdrew her cell phone and called the task force, placing it on speakerphone.

"We have a problem," Walsh said in greeting.

"How'd you know?" Elijah asked.

"Penny is in critical condition," Walsh said, answering Elijah and ignoring him at the same time.

"How? We were just there," Tiandra replied.

"We're watching her hospital files online," Eliana said. "According to the medical records, something was injected into her IV line. A nurse found the unlabeled vial on the floor, and the doctors are struggling to counteract the chemical."

"Wow." Tiandra sighed.

"It was the woman I chased through the hospital." Elijah explained the events. "The nurse ran out hollering for a doctor."

"That explains why," Eliana added.

"Penny started to tell me who hurt her when someone tackled me from behind," Tiandra said, "and knocked me out."

"Get to Skyler. She's waiting with Bosco," Walsh instructed. "We'll monitor Penny's progress."

"We should connect with Mikko," Elijah said. "Either he ordered the hit on us, or things are amping up."

"Agreed. We're getting tackled at every turn," Tiandra replied. "Someone's got an agenda and we're interrupting it."

"Keep the faith," Walsh said.

They disconnected and arrived to meet Skyler in record time.

Tiandra and Elijah changed from the disguises into their normal clothing. Skyler tossed the bag into her car.

"Someone wants to make sure Penny doesn't talk," Tiandra said as she slipped into her jacket.

Skyler shook her head. "Maybe you should call it quits."

"Negative," Tiandra said. "Elijah is welcome to go if it's too much, but all this is doing is telling me we're super close to finishing this case."

"I'm with Tiandra," Elijah said.

Under no circumstance would he leave her alone to handle the situation.

"Be careful," Skyler said, walking into the restaurant and leaving them with Bosco.

The Malinois thumped his tail at their approach, clearly grateful to reunite with his partner. Elijah reached to greet the dog, stroking his head and velvety ears. "We missed you too," he whispered.

They transferred Bosco from Skyler's car to the pickup before heading toward Mikko's home.

"How do we explain the vehicle change?" Elijah asked.

"Tell him we took the truck. He'll assume we stole it, which should satisfy him," Tiandra said.

"Good idea."

"My mind is spinning with possibilities. We requested to go to the hideout, but did Mikko agree with the intention of baiting us with the low-level gangsters before sending in the 29 Locos Cartel? Or did they respond after learning we were there?" Tiandra groaned, resting her head against the headrest.

"How're you feeling?" Elijah reached over, intending to touch her arm, then quickly retracted his hand. *Know your place.*

"Better. But I'm kicking myself. Why didn't I discern someone was there with me? My instincts are stronger than that."

"I failed too. That woman got away because of me."

"You're certain it was a woman?" Tiandra asked.

"Absolutely."

"Did you recognize her?"

"Not really. Like I said, from a distance, she resembled you."

"Great." Tiandra's phone rang. "It's Walsh." She quickly answered.

"Tiandra, you and Elijah stay low," Walsh said in greeting. "Stay away from Mikko."

Did the man ever start with hello?

"Just got a call from the locals," he continued. "They're looking for a woman who fits your profile. She's wanted for questioning."

"What? Why?"

"The hospital security tapes show footage of a woman resembling you entering Penny's room," Riker said. "Eliana is working on obtaining a copy of the video, and Walsh is trying to hold up the release of it to law enforcement."

Tiandra blinked, eyes fixed on Elijah. "Wait, it shows me?"

"No, you were in disguise. It displays a woman who looks like you. Brown hair, street clothes," Walsh clarified.

"Does it show Elijah too?" Tiandra asked.

"No," Walsh said. "It appears that part was eliminated with time lapse."

"Someone doctored the footage?" Tiandra gasped. "My assailant framed me for Penny's attack?"

FIFTEEN

The day after the hospital visit, Tiandra paced the offsite office space where her teammates sat in chairs around the metal table. Walsh had ordered an in-person meeting for the team, untrusting of electronic communications after the video footage debacle. The commander's talent at finding remote locations was unsurpassed, as the current BOO confirmed. The under-construction building seventy-five miles from the Kings' decimated hideout, in what Tiandra would describe as no-man's-land, South Dakota, offered them safety from Mikko's radar. It also gave Tiandra and Elijah a place to lodge with backup.

"I can't believe the way this is spinning out," Tiandra said. "How do we go from an ordered hit on Graham to Elijah and I being gunned down at the hideout, then someone trying to set me up for attempted murder?"

"If you hadn't shown up when you did, Penny would already be dead," Riker replied.

Skyler dropped to sit at the table. "She owes you her life, even if she doesn't know it."

"Except I'm in law enforcement's crosshairs for a crime I didn't commit," Tiandra whined, hating herself for crumbling under the stress and unable to stop it.

Eliana's large mobile computer monitor replayed the footage from the hospital, depicting a woman resembling Tiandra, sans the disguise she wore that day, slipping undetected into Penny's room just seconds before Tiandra entered. The team had worked endlessly to analyze the material, but the attacker had brilliantly kept the video from capturing her face while ensuring the rest of her appearance mimicked Tiandra. As though she wanted to be recognized enough to set up Tiandra while not identifying herself. Or as the prosecution would present the case, without reasonable doubt.

"How did we miss her?" Tiandra asked, leaning closer to the screen.

"She must've followed you there," Chance said, "and waited for the perfect opportunity."

"Her timing is impeccable, not coincidental," Riker agreed.

"I've dug through everything I could get my hands on," Eliana said. "There's nothing showing you and Elijah entering the hospital or Penny's room, or departing."

"Here's what I don't understand." Elijah joined the discussion. "We wore disguises. They couldn't have known it was us. So how did they know when to delete the footage?"

"They were watching," Skyler said. "Anticipating your arrival."

"They probably weren't certain it was you at

first," Eliana added. "We're talking two or more criminals working to coordinate this."

"Once Tiandra entered Penny's room, they had confirmation," Chance said.

"Have they discovered what the attacker injected Penny with?" Tiandra asked.

"No," Walsh said. "And until they do, her life is in jeopardy." He strode to the door and exited, cell phone pressed to his ear.

"Why frame Tiandra?" Chance asked.

"To get me out of the way," Tiandra replied.

Walsh returned, still holding the phone. His grim expression quieted the team as they eavesdropped on his conversation. "Understood. Thank you for the extra time." He dropped the device into his shirt pocket.

"I'm afraid to ask," Tiandra said as he joined them at the table.

"The video is condemning," Walsh began.

"But I—"

"And—" Walsh lifted a disapproving eyebrow to silence her "—I cannot stop law enforcement from viewing the hospital video."

Eliana glanced up from her computer screen. "I've issued a request to law enforcement to withhold it from the media, as per your instruction, Commander."

"Good." Walsh nodded. "I spoke with my boss, and he agrees we have a limited time before the vultures descend."

"What motive could I possibly have for trying to kill Penny?" Tiandra asked.

"They'll spin it any way they want," Riker said. The group grew solemn, recalling Riker's battle to prove his innocence after being framed by his twin. "The investigation must be without reproach. Trust me when I say I get how hard it is to just sit and watch while you wait to be exonerated."

"Ugh," Tiandra groaned. "We're caught between a rock and an impossible place. If we tell the police Elijah and I were there disguised, we compromise our undercover roles. If we don't, I look guilty."

"We've got your back," Walsh said.

"Yeah," Riker nodded. "We need to be the first to talk to Penny when she awakens. It can't be you, Tiandra. You have to stay away from the hospital until we find out more."

"Yes," Walsh said. "We can't interfere with the current investigation from local law enforcement, but we're keeping close watch on Penny."

"I'll keep you all up to date by the minute," Skyler said. "On that same note—"

Chance's cell phone rang. "Be right back." He rose and excused himself from the room. His K-9, Destiny, lifted her head, ears perked, then lay down again at his departure. She'd grown comfortable with the group.

Skyler continued, "Graham's condition has improved, but he remains unconscious. The doctors feel that's good as the time allows reduction in his brain swelling."

Tiandra met Elijah's worried expression. Everything within her longed to comfort him, but nothing short of hearing Graham was in full recovery would accomplish that. She also wanted to reach out, embrace him, or at the very least hold his hand, but that would raise questions with the team, and she couldn't put them under that kind of scrutiny. Not that anyone would condemn them. Riker had fallen in love with his wife, Eliana, during their investigation and they were happily married. Annoyingly blissful and enamored with each other. Chance and Ayla, the witness he'd protected, were newlyweds. It seemed romance encircled the group, except for her.

A loneliness Tiandra hadn't expected overwhelmed her as she grasped how many of her teammates were finding joy in love. Would she ever know that, especially if she was incarcerated? Something she'd never considered before had become a possibility she had no control to stop.

"How does Penny fit into this?" Walsh asked the team.

Tiandra blinked, realizing she'd zoned out on part of the conversation.

"Penny is the key, but until she tells us anything, if she does, we continue working clues and leads," Tiandra said. "She's covering for Mikko. Her comment about love protects explains that."

"Absolutely," Elijah added. "He's got serious control over her."

"She's protecting Mikko from what? Penny never named Graham per se, but she kept saying 'grr.'" Tiandra rose and paced by the evidence board. "If she's made us, did Mikko set up the attack at the hideout to kill us?"

"That's plausible. Eliminate you both in a two-for-one attack." Riker leaned back, crossing his leg over his knee. "If he ordered the hit."

"No, I don't buy it," Elijah argued. "He had a hundred opportunities to kill me and Tiandra while we were under his roof."

Tiandra dropped to her seat and rested her forehead on her crossed arms on the table. "This is unreal."

Chance returned and resumed his place at the table. "Sorry to interrupt, but I have a lead."

"Speak, man!" Riker urged him.

"What if you go a different direction?" Chance asked, gaining the group's attention.

"Like?" Elijah gestured with his hand for Chance to continue.

"Just spoke with the DEA." Chance slid a piece of paper across the table. "After a lot of discussion, being transferred a hundred times, and finally promising my and Ayla's first-born child," he joked, referring to his new bride, "I have confirmed that the number Eliana got off Graham's cell phone matches a DEA task force case Graham worked before joining HFTF."

Tiandra glanced at Chance's chicken scratch on the document. "Um, I can't read that."

Elijah slid it closer and studied the paper. "You sure you weren't supposed to be a doctor? What does that say?"

Chance's cheeks reddened. "Really? Okay, Graham's DEA task force spent two years putting the evidence together to take down major drug runners working St. Louis, Minneapolis, Denver, and Omaha." He dropped into a chair. "Turns out Graham was involved in a sting where he shot and killed one of the dealers. The after-action report deemed it a clean shot."

"Interesting. What's the connection to this investigation?" Tiandra asked.

"Yeah, that many years after the fact can't involve the same players," Elijah added.

"This." Chance waved the paper. "It's the list of those involved in the sting. We can start digging through each one for any link to the current case."

"Outstanding work," Walsh said.

Elijah rose and walked to the evidence board where a map of South Dakota and Nebraska hung, pierced by pins indicating prior Kings' activity and locations. "Has anyone else noticed how the tacks seem to make a pattern?"

The team joined him, reviewing the map.

"Look here." Elijah pointed to a section between

the state borders. "The Kings have a way of choosing areas within this circle." He used his finger to draw on the map. "Mikko is thorough about spreading out the players and the locations, while he's consistent with keeping within this specific radius. He stays in the rural regions. But see how there's a bald spot here?"

"Yes." Tiandra inched closer, brushing against Elijah's arm. "It's so blank it stands out."

"Right?" Elijah turned to face her. "This rural land offers him the opportunity to do his work undetected. Plus, it's on the Nebraska side of the South Dakota border."

Walsh nodded. "We've focused primarily on South Dakota, but the commute isn't out of the question. They could easily travel back and forth in a day's time."

"Precisely." Elijah dropped onto a chair at the table. "I keep thinking about that paper I found at the barn. If there was litter around it, I wouldn't give it a second thought, but it was so out of place. The only paper on the floor. It means something."

The group gave a collective groan, but their faces revealed good-natured teasing. They'd discussed the find with a hundred different thoughts and still came up empty.

"Blurt out ideas, people," Chance said, holding a blue dry erase marker in front of the whiteboard.

"It's a legal document," Skyler said.

"Instructions," Tiandra said.

"A receipt," Riker added.

"Like for something from a car. Maybe tires," Eliana said.

Chance wrote the words as they called them out.

"All good ideas." Walsh paced the perimeter of the room. He stopped and examined the paper again. "It's smeared and hard to read, but there are distinct letters at the top right above the ripped half. *O-k-s-t-o-n.*"

"A business logo or header?" Tiandra asked, interest piquing.

Eliana typed furiously on her keyboard. "I'm not finding any businesses using those letters near the barn where you found it, Elijah."

"Expound the search into northern Nebraska and Iowa, the closest bordering states," Riker suggested.

Eliana continued typing. "Hmm, there's a Brookston Bakery coming up in Nebraska."

"Yes!" Elijah jumped up and rushed to Eliana. "Where did you say Mikko's family farm was?"

"Just outside Valentine, Nebraska."

"Please pull up a map of northern Nebraska and zoom in." Elijah leaned closer. "Look for smaller towns or villages that aren't showing on the wall map."

Eliana did as he asked, the others joining them, and hovering around her.

"It's rural. Nothing except farms," Skyler mumbled.

"That's it!" Elijah pointed at the screen, then

slammed his hand on the table. The team members looked at him with concern and confusion etched in their startled expressions. "Sorry, but it's totally coming together for me. Mikko's family owned property in Valentine, which is near Brookston! And I'm guessing there's a grain elevator."

They nodded, obviously still puzzled.

"Don't you see?" Elijah pointed to the paper. "It's a receipt!"

Eliana tapped away. "He's right. There's a grain elevator in that area."

"It makes sense," Elijah continued. "They are often located near railways and waterways to accommodate shipping the grain after it's processed."

"A great way to haul drugs undetected!" Riker added. "Dude, that's brilliant."

Elijah smiled widely, and Tiandra couldn't help but notice how he soaked up the praise.

"Let's check it out," Tiandra said, pushing back from the table. "I can't just sit here. I have to do something."

"Not a bad idea," Walsh agreed. "It gets you two out of the area while we deal with the hospital security video."

"There's gotta be some evidence to prove it's not me." She glanced at Riker, one of the few members of the group who truly understood her predicament after his own framing encounter. He gave her an understanding nod.

"We got your six," he said, referencing the cop

slang for having her back. "More importantly, God has this. He knows exactly what we need to prove the attacker isn't you."

"We'll find it," Walsh assured. "All right, team, let's work the leads." He stood. "After we pray."

The group huddled, lifting their voices and petitions.

Peace settled over Tiandra. With God's help, her task force family would ensure justice was had. They had to, because anything less meant she'd be charged with attempted murder and Elijah's killer would eliminate him.

The sun had almost set by the time Elijah drove the four-door sedan over the railroad tracks, crossing onto the grain elevator property. They'd traveled clear streets, though snow drifts bordered the county road into Nebraska. "I sure hope this pans out," he said.

The 120-foot-tall ginormous structure loomed in the distance, its white cement exterior boring and nondescript.

"Is that it?" Tiandra scooted to the edge of her seat and pointed.

"That's the one." Elijah aimed for the grain elevator and parked in front of it. "Let's see if we find anything."

Tiandra faced him. "Wait, before we go inside, I need to ask you to do something for me."

Her seriousness concerned Elijah, and he shut off the engine. "Sure."

"If this goes wrong, and I end up going to jail for Penny—"

"You won't," he interrupted.

"Hear me out."

"Okay, sorry."

Tiandra glanced down and audibly swallowed. Her voice was tight and everything within Elijah fought to not pull her into his arms. "Please finish the investigation and takedown Graham's attacker."

"Definitely," Elijah assured.

"And," Tiandra continued, "arrest the Kings. Those drugs cannot hit the streets."

Elijah studied Tiandra. Her first concern wasn't in her exoneration and possible incarceration. Instead, she focused on justice for Graham and the goal of destroying the Kings.

Everything about Tiandra Daugherty intrigued him. And in that moment, Elijah realized whatever it took, he'd honor her request. "Of course," he replied lamely. *That's it? That's the best you can think of?* His internal critic slammed accusations, but words eluded him.

What he wanted to say most was that he'd fallen head over heels for Tiandra. And that was the one confession he could not make. Not now. Not ever. Especially with Graham's life hanging in the balance and his full awareness that his brother was also in love with Tiandra. For once, he agreed with

Graham. She was everything Elijah had dreamed of, and he hated his poor timing in not meeting her first.

"Are you okay?" Tiandra touched his arm, brows furrowed.

"Um, yeah. Just got a lot on my mind," Elijah said absently. Did that sound like a brush-off? "We must get this case solved. You cannot go to jail," he quickly added.

"Let's hope it doesn't come to that." Tiandra looked down. "I'm a realist. These things sometimes go wrong. I want to be prepared for the worst."

Elijah understood completely, though it changed nothing in his mind or resolve. Whatever it took, he'd make sure Tiandra wasn't convicted.

They exited the car, and Tiandra leashed Bosco.

"You don't think he'll stay by us without the leash?" Elijah asked.

"He probably would, but it's precautionary, so he doesn't get hurt."

"That makes sense," Elijah said.

They paused, glancing up at the massive metal-and-concrete structure.

"I can honestly say I've never considered entering one of these," Tiandra said. "I know nothing about grain elevators."

"Here's my chance to amaze you with my masterful knowledge," Elijah said, taking a silly bow. "They harvest the grain—mainly soybeans and corn—in the fall and bring it here to store. After it's sampled and weighed, they put it on the conveyor belt and drop it by a bucket system into the silos."

"Aha, a word I recognize," Tiandra teased.

Elijah pointed to the facility. "They store the grain before it is transported. There's a lot more to it, but that gives you the gist."

"I am impressed." Tiandra grinned. "So it's only open in the spring, summer, and fall?"

"The elevator is accessible year-round."

Five matching cylindrical buildings connected to the tallest of the infrastructure shaped like a tin house with a narrower version of the same at the top. Rust stains poured from the windows of the base building, and skinny ladders clung to the sides.

They walked to the main door where a printed sign read, *Closed until January. Happy Holidays.*

"That explains the lack of personnel," Tiandra said.

"Let's see if there's a side entrance." Elijah led the way around and tugged at a metal door. "Locked."

"Now what?"

"Watch." He held up his keyring, revealing a small lock pick.

Tiandra lifted one brow.

"Don't ask," he said.

With a few twists of the tool, Elijah released the lock with a satisfying click. He smiled and reached for the door, tugging it open. The metal hinges screeched disapproval as they entered.

"Let's not turn on the overhead lights," Elijah said.

"Agreed. Think there are cameras here?"

"Doubtful, but we don't need any unwanted company right now while we're snooping."

Tiandra withdrew and flicked on a flashlight from her back pocket, slicing the darkened space with light. The concrete floors were dusty, and the odor of rotten soybeans mingled with dampness and mold.

"Ew." Tiandra covered her mouth with her sleeve.

"Rancid, right?"

"I've worked crime scenes that smelled better than this." She lowered her arm and wrinkled her nose, the action making her beautiful face more attractive.

Elijah averted his eyes and shook off the thought. "Rotting grain has a distinct odor," he said. *Brilliant deduction.*

"Oh, good. For a second I worried we were in the wrong place," Tiandra teased.

Their feet echoed on the concrete as they maneuvered through the dank main floor.

She grinned and passed him, moving through the walkway of the empty confined lower level. There were no obvious signs of life, but the absence of people argued with Elijah's instincts, which said someone was there recently.

"You think Mikko's using this place?" Tiandra asked, her voice soft but the reverberations carrying in the cavernous space.

"Possibly. This might be the location for the deal,

especially with the building being closed for the holidays," Elijah said, stating the obvious.

"My thoughts exactly." Tiandra paused by a partially open door with a sign that read *Basement Tunnels*, and peeked inside. "Not gonna lie. That doesn't look inviting."

"But it's a great place to hide drugs," Elijah said. "I'll check it out and holler if there's anything worth seeing."

"No way, I'm not leaving you without backup." Tiandra lifted her chin defiantly and strangely adorable.

Elijah shifted closer, his arm brushing her side. Using every bit of strength, he forced himself not to react to the touch, though being that close to her was exhilarating. He cleared his throat and glanced down at the steep steps that led downward in a plunging drop. "Can Bosco walk down those?"

"Yes, but it won't be easy," Tiandra said, but her tone was not convincing. "Up would be easier on him."

Elijah surveyed the canine, recalling images of military personnel carrying their dogs over their shoulders. "He won't have to do either. I'll carry him, if you think he'll let me."

"Bosco, here." He moved to her side.

Elijah bent down, gently lifting the dog and placing him over his neck and shoulders, then secured him by holding on to his paws. "Okay, lead on, but go slow."

They descended the steps, Tiandra clinging to the railing to keep from falling.

When they reached the bottom, Elijah set Bosco on the cold floor. He gave a thorough shake of his fur.

Tiandra swept the flashlight beam across the cement catacomb. "This place is creepy."

Elijah didn't answer, but he wholeheartedly agreed.

They strode through the basement, the concrete walls closing in on them. The grain elevator buckets hung from the conveyer belt in a too-still silence. A chill ran down his back. "There's nothing here."

"Yep." Tiandra spun on her heel. "Let's get upstairs."

"Bosco, mind if I carry you?" Elijah knelt beside the Malinois.

A quick tail swishing confirmed Bosco's approval and he hoisted the dog onto his shoulders again. Tiandra led the way as they ascended the steps to the main floor. Finding nothing there, they moved toward the metal elevator and tugged open the accordion door, revealing the small cube interior.

She lifted a brow. "You want me to get inside that?"

"We need to check out the headhouse."

At her confused expression, Elijah clarified, "The upper part of the main building."

"That would provide Mikko the high ground and advantage should anyone approach."

"Precisely." Elijah studied the metal structure. "It'll be a tight fit."

They entered the elevator, squeezing close together in the confining space. Elijah tugged closed the accordion door and turned the switch. With a creak and a rumble, they ascended.

"Yep, this is how I'm going to die, squished in an iron cube as I plunge to my death," Tiandra said sarcastically.

"Nah, we're completely safe." Elijah grinned, but the rattling of the old structure did nothing to help his argument.

When they reached the upper level, he released the latch, and they exited the elevator into the windowless and stuffy headhouse.

Together, they searched the space.

"I doubt they'd use the silos, but we could check those out too." Elijah led the way through the hall toward the massive bins.

Tiandra paused. "I didn't notice this door," she said, nuzzling the ajar door open. "Do you smell that?"

"Didn't we just cover this topic?" Elijah teased.

She swatted at his arm. "No, it's different. Sweet. Out of place here."

Elijah inhaled deeply, realizing his mistake as the tickle enveloped his nose, launching him into a sneezing fit. After the last one, he sheepishly looked at Tiandra. "So much for sneaking in. Sorry."

She chuckled. "Not like you could help it. I didn't mean for you to have an allergy attack. I just thought I got a hint of perfume. Smells like the brand one of my sisters wears."

Elijah's nostrils were filled with the rotting grain scent, but he nodded. "My mom always smells stuff I can't," he admitted.

"I guess we're just born with better sniffers." She jerked her chin at Bosco. "Although he beats us all."

"No doubt." Elijah shifted and held out an arm, gesturing toward the narrow walkway. "You first. Let your nose lead on."

She entered and Elijah trailed her, propping the door open with one foot. "I don't want us to get locked in here. Might be years before anyone found us," he whispered. Boxes and furniture littered the large space, void of windows or light.

Tiandra disappeared behind a bulky metal file cabinet.

"Check this out." Her flashlight swept the room.

Elijah remained by the door, searching for something to keep it open. He spotted an old gray iron chair. "Hey, would you push that to me?"

Tiandra did as he asked.

After securing the chair, he followed her around the cabinet. There, a thick foam mattress pad with a sleeping bag occupied the corner. Beside the makeshift bed, a lamp sat atop a small box. Bosco moved forward, actively sniffing, and paused, glancing at Tiandra as though conveying some silent message.

She released his leash, passing the flashlight to Elijah. Then she knelt next to the dog, gently lifting the lamp, and lifted the box lid.

Elijah shone the light inside, revealing a sizable stash of dollar bills secured with a paper wrapper and an old Polaroid picture.

"What do we have here?"

"Wow, I haven't seen one of these photos in years," he said, using his T-shirt sleeve to withdraw the picture. If there were any fingerprints on it, he'd not destroy them. He lifted it to the light. The Polaroid depicted a teen boy holding a little girl's hand as they posed in front of a Christmas tree. Both smiled wide. A few meager, wrapped gifts lay at the base of the tree, which was covered in homemade ornaments and a paper chain garland. The quality lacked clarity, leaving the details indistinct.

The boy's pants appeared dirty and too short, with holes at the knees. He wore high-top athletic sneakers. The girl's dress was too tight, with a large stain across the front. She wore two different-colored Mary Jane shoes. Neither seemed bothered by their deficient atmosphere.

"They look happy," Tiandra said softly. "And strangely familiar."

"Do you think it's Mikko?" Elijah asked.

"No, but maybe Penny. The girl has the same dirty blonde hair. But I can't tell what color her eyes are." Tiandra continued studying the Polaroid. "She lost her brother, Hank, when they were young."

"If it's not Penny, who else is it?"

"Good question." She surveyed the room. "I can't believe someone would be brave enough to live here."

"It's vacant and provides shelter. I've seen squatters and homeless people reside in worse conditions," Elijah said.

"I guess. It's kind of sad. But they would've known the place was closed for the holidays," Tiandra said.

Elijah swept the beam across the floor. "I'm surprised at the amount of grain dust lying around here."

"Isn't that expected, considering the work they do here?"

Elijah shook his head. "Grain dust is highly flammable. Maintenance is a must to mitigate any possible explosions."

"It explodes?" Tiandra asked, her tone unbelieving.

"Big time."

"Wow. I'd never have guessed that." Tiandra set the Polaroid on the sleeping bag and snapped a picture with her cell phone. "I'll see if the team can track it down somehow. Eliana is great at finding clues. Maybe there's something here—"

Bosco barked, calling their attention to the sound of a large engine roaring to life.

SIXTEEN

"What is that noise?" Tiandra shoved her cell phone into her pocket and withdrew her Glock from her waistband.

"The conveyer belt." Elijah drew his weapon, and they rushed to the door. He whipped the chair out of the way. "We have to get out of here. Now."

Tiandra didn't argue based on the urgency in his voice and expression. They hurried from the room to the elevator doors, standing open.

Along with Bosco, they crammed into the confining space and Elijah gripped the door, tugging it closed. He shifted the latch.

Nothing happened.

He repeated the maneuver several times, each effort more desperate than the first. "Someone cut the power."

"What do we do now?" Tiandra held Bosco close to her side.

"Climb down." Elijah shoved open the accordion doors. "If the dust on that conveyer belt ignites, it'll create a massive explosion."

The implication struck Tiandra. Somebody intended to trap them in the headhouse and burn them to death.

"We're over a hundred feet in the sky. How do

we get down?" Tiandra inhaled slow, deep breaths to combat the panic squeezing her chest.

Elijah looked at Bosco. "We'll have to use the external ladders."

"You've gotta be kidding."

"There's no other way down."

Tiandra gulped. "But Bosco—"

"I'll carry him." Elijah squatted and gently lifted Bosco, placing him over his shoulders in military style.

Tiandra followed Elijah, quickening her pace. *Lord, help us.*

Grinding and clattering of the conveyer belt echoed in the space with an eerie and terrifying moan.

Elijah walked to a narrow door and opened it. The cold winter air drifted inside, and they crawled out to where the ladder clung to the side of the silo. "I'll go first. Careful, steady steps," he instructed.

Tiandra nodded mutely. "What if the person is waiting for us below?"

"Let's focus on getting down, okay?" Elijah turned, one hand bracing Bosco's paws around his neck, draped like a scarf, the other holding on to the ladder.

They slowly descended. Tiandra's hands gripped the cold metal with a desperation born of terror. The winter wind whipped against her face. She squeezed her eyes to create moisture and refused to look down.

The climb seemed to take forever, though they moved with matched precision down the ladder.

A boom had Tiandra momentarily pausing. She met Elijah's terrified eyes. "What was that?" Her question was consumed by the echoes of the loud noise.

"Get down!" Elijah hollered.

His urgency confused Tiandra at first. "Why? What's wrong?"

"Let go!" Elijah released his hold and Tiandra gasped as he jumped to the earth below. "Let go!" he cried again.

Though she was nearly six feet from the ground she mimicked his move and landed hard in an exaggerated squat to lessen the impact. Her boots crunched on the gravel.

"Run!" Elijah urged, setting down Bosco.

Tiandra read his lips, unable to hear past her drumming pulse that overwhelmed her senses.

Elijah grabbed her hand, and with Bosco beside her, they sprinted from the building. "Keep going!" he hollered.

They reached a considerable distance before a second boom erupted. Tiandra comprehended both were explosions.

"Get to the car." Elijah's voice permeated the ringing in her ears.

The tall silo buildings left too many hiding places for a shooter. Their vehicle was on the other side, which forced them to cross the open area uncovercd. Without another option, they sprinted across the ground and lunged for the sedan, diving inside. Elijah took the driver's seat and Tiandra jerked closed the door even as they sped from the property. Debris rained around them and Elijah swerved on the road to avoid being hit or colliding with the cement and metal.

Another explosion detonated behind them.

"Someone didn't appreciate our intrusion." Tiandra twisted around, watching the dust and smoke billowing into the sky. Bosco whined, standing on the backseat. "Are you okay?" He licked her hand, and she stroked his ears. "You did good, buddy."

When they'd crossed the road, a subsequent explosion rocked the earth.

Tiandra stared at the building, now consumed in clouds and flames that illuminated the atmosphere. Baffled, she gaped and turned to Elijah. "Did they set a bomb? A trap for us?"

"Remember, grain dust is highly explosive. It wouldn't take much to start a fire. Then each subsequent blast is worse than the first."

Confirming Elijah's words, part of the headhouse tumbled to the ground. With shaking hands she called Commander Walsh.

"What'd you find?" he asked in greeting.

"A grain explosion." Tiandra launched into an abridged explanation of their experience.

"Unreal. Get back to the BOO."

"Roger that." Tiandra hung up and shared the information with Elijah.

"I should've taken the box with the picture and money."

"I texted the photo to the team, so we have some record."

"I grabbed this." Elijah withdrew a dust-covered piece of orange fabric from his jacket pocket.

"Where did you find that?"

"On the ground by the ladder."

Tiandra had been so consumed by the treacherous descent and jump that she'd never seen him do it. She examined the fabric, stretching it flat on her leg and flipped on the overhead light. "There's a number two written in black marker on here."

"I thought it was some sort of design," Elijah said.

Tiandra shook her head. "Nope, the 29 Locos Cartel gives these orange bandanas to high-level players. Whoever was living in there was a gang member."

"Are you sure?"

"Definitely."

"So, the insider works for the cartel and Mikko? Is that what Penny tried to tell us?"

Tiandra considered the last two times she'd talked to the woman. She contemplated her former partner's strange behavior combined with what Elijah had told her about Graham's personal feelings for her. Should she share her suspicions with him?

"Okay, talk," Elijah said, no doubt seeing she was deep in thought.

"I was working through the clues in my head."

"Let's do that together."

She hesitated. "But what if I say something you don't like?"

"Try me."

"Penny kept saying 'grr,' at the hospital. I assumed she meant Graham."

"We discussed that with the team," he reminded her.

"Sort of." Tiandra sucked in a breath. "Or Graham was in cahoots with Mikko."

"You think my brother was dirty?"

Tiandra prayed for wisdom. "I did at one time, but now I'm wondering if it's something else. When he went to Walsh, Graham mentioned a woman getting in the way. I assumed he referred to me. What if he meant Penny?"

"That's totally plausible."

"Right? It explains a lot."

"Or 'grr' as in grain elevator," Elijah said.

"Why'd you have to go there?" Tiandra groaned, leaning back. "Now that also makes sense." In the side mirror she watched as the elevator inferno raged. "She knows who the insider is."

They traveled to the county highway. Darkness had descended, covering them in shadows with only the car's headlights illuminating a path.

"True confession," Tiandra began. "I misjudged

Graham. Totally judged, sentenced, the whole kit and caboodle."

Elijah laughed. "Now there's a term I haven't heard since my grandparents were around."

"Are you saying I'm old?"

"Never."

She grinned. "Graham probably suspected Penny was onto something, but he wasn't sure. I had this whole scenario worked out in my mind about how he wanted me kicked off the investigation because he didn't think I could do the job. Then you told me about his feelings for me. I had him pegged all wrong."

Elijah grabbed her hand, surprising Tiandra. She stiffened, and he withdrew his touch, wearing an apologetic expression. "You went with the information you had. Now you know differently."

Tiandra hung her head. "I never realized how much my resentment hindered my faith. I felt like I had steel prayers that floated to the ceiling and slammed down on my head. My judgmental attitude created a barrier between me, Graham, and God."

"What should you do?"

"Forgive Graham. Whatever reason he had for not sharing the intel had to have been justifiable. He was working the case, and I was focused on nursing my emotions."

Elijah squeezed her shoulder. "Forgive yourself too. We all make mistakes."

"I guess." She shook her head. "I'll add that to my list of reconcilations."

Elijah tilted his head, confused.

"My sister Meghan. She's tried reaching out to me, and I've avoided her. It's time we made up."

"Good plan," Elijah replied. "When Graham wakes up, you can give him the whole story and impress his socks off. He's given us the clues we need. We'll put it together."

"Agreed." Tiandra smiled. "For Graham."

The idea hit Elijah between the eyes. "Call the task force back," he blurted.

"Now?"

"Yes, please."

Tiandra dialed as he pulled onto the shoulder.

"What's wrong?" Walsh asked.

"I have to meet with Mikko," Elijah blurted, watching Tiandra's cell phone as though he could see the team on the minuscule screen.

"We'll discuss it when you arrive," Walsh said.

"Negative," Elijah replied. "Sir, with all due respect—"

"He hates when people use that phrase," Tiandra whispered.

Elijah winced. "Sir, we don't have time. We need to get to Mikko ASAP."

"I hate to agree with him," Riker said, "but if the grain elevator was the planned drug deal location, that's over now. We have nothing else to go on."

"Okay, but how do we do that given Penny's and Tiandra's situations?" Skyler asked.

"I go in alone," Elijah replied.

The sadness in Tiandra's eyes tore at him. "He's right. And if he plays it off correctly, he'll be able to answer for my absence."

"And it should give us the information we need to determine what side Mikko is on in this whole mess," Chance replied.

"Okay," Walsh said, to Elijah's surprise. He'd fully expected the commander to dismiss his idea.

"He could wear a wire," Eliana offered.

"No way," Tiandra refuted. "Mikko would kill him without question if he found it."

Elijah inwardly cringed. "I'll make contact and Tiandra will keep you updated. Let me get that first meeting in."

A collective agreement allowed him to proceed with his plan.

"I'll leave a vehicle for Tiandra at location four," Skyler said, using the code they'd established prior to the grain elevator visit.

"Roger that."

They disconnected.

"Are you sure about this?" Tiandra asked.

"Yes. Strike while the iron is exploding," Elijah said, then using his undercover cell, he called Mikko.

"Where you been?" Mikko barked.

"Hiding out," Elijah replied. "Heat's on."

"Yeah? Why?"

The man was clearly baiting him. Testing him. "I'm not talking on the phone. Let's meet."

"Where?"

"You pick."

"Keystone. I'll text instructions from there," Mikko said, disconnecting.

Tiandra sighed. "He's going to take you on a wild goose chase before he gives you the location."

"Where will you be?"

"Don't worry about us. Bosco and I are cool."

They completed the drive to where Tiandra and Elijah would part ways. He pulled up to the old service garage beside a parked car. Tiandra pushed open her door, sadness lingering in her smile. Elijah clung to the wheel to keep from pulling her close. He wanted to protect her. How could he do that without arresting Mikko? They'd never be safe until Mikko and the killer were behind bars. Separating from her was the next necessary step, even though it killed him to do so.

"See you at Lovers Leap at 2309," she said, leaving the car. The meeting location and time provided him some reassurance. She opened the passenger rear door and Bosco hopped out, joining her.

Elijah watched, helpless to stop Tiandra as she entered the adjacent vehicle and started the engine. With a wave, she drove off ahead of him as planned.

"Please, God, take care of her. Help us finish

this," he prayed aloud, turning onto the road and heading to Keystone.

When he reached the city limits, he texted Mikko, who provided a mile marker meeting place. Elijah headed to the location and texted again. Mikko continued the game for several miles, his final message leading Elijah to Custer State Park where he parked in front of a simple cabin. A soft light glowed from the window.

Had Tiandra followed him, watching from a distance? He shut off the engine and slid out of the car. Maintaining a confident stride, he approached the ajar door and rapped twice.

"Come on in, G," Mikko said.

Elijah inhaled and entered the log structure, his boots thudding on the hardwood floor. Mikko sat near the wall, his Sig aimed at Elijah.

"Look, man, I don't know what's up, but if you're going to shoot me, just do it. I've been burned at every level, and I'm done," Elijah said.

"How's that?" Mikko quirked a disbelieving brow.

"What'd I tell you about women?" Elijah asked, baiting the criminal. "No matter what they say, they'll spin on a dime and stab you in the back."

"What're you rambling about?" Mikko feigned disinterest, but Elijah saw the curiosity in his expression.

"She played me!" Elijah infused anger into his tone. "I told you I'd bolt if I had an inkling."

"Tia?" Mikko was no actor.

Elijah read him easily and acted accordingly. He was fully aware of the situation with Penny and Tiandra.

"I almost died!"

Mikko lowered the gun. "You wearing a wire?"

"Dude, really?" Elijah ripped off his jacket and shirt and turned. "See anything?"

In the corner, another Kings member stepped from the shadows, and for a second, Elijah wondered if he'd made a horrible mistake.

"Check him out," Mikko ordered.

The unfamiliar man patted Elijah down, examining for wires, and withdrew the Glock from his waistband then handed it to Mikko. "He's clean except for this."

"Sit down," Mikko demanded, placing the weapon on the table beside him.

Elijah tugged on his shirt and jacket, then dropped onto the chair opposite Mikko. The other man disappeared into the shadows again, no doubt keeping his weapon trained on Elijah.

Mikko stood, his pistol centered on Elijah. "So, am I supposed to believe you didn't know your girlfriend is a Fed?"

Elijah blinked, comprehending Mikko's words. Tiandra's cover was blown. Was his? He met the man's icy gaze, maintaining a steady reply. "Not my problem what you believe."

Mikko tilted his head, the weapon unwavering. "Did you play me?"

"Why do that and come here to die?"

Mikko's sardonic guffaw filled the room. "That would be especially stupid."

"Exactly."

"All right." Mikko lowered the gun and returned to sit across from Elijah again. "What are you willing to do to prove it to me?"

"Name it."

"I need verification that you're telling me the truth. You understand I can't just take your word for it."

Elijah shrugged. "What else do I have?"

"I must trust my men. Gotta assume they are who they say they are. How can I do that now with this most recent development?"

"Look, man, I came here telling you Tia played me. 29 Locos chased after me and I nearly died escaping them. I've proven my loyalty over and over. What do you want from me? I'm here because I'm committed. Period."

"Hmm…perhaps." Mikko tapped the tip of the gun against his lips in mock consideration. "The deal is going down. I don't have time to vet a new partner."

"You don't need to." Elijah scooted to the edge of his chair. "I'm here. Let's do it."

"Yes." Mikko met his gaze. His eyes, so dark they were almost black, leaving his pupils indistinguishable from his irises, bore into Elijah. A coldness consumed them with such intensity, ice shivered down Elijah's spine. This was a cold-blooded killer waiting to take him out. "Just one requirement before we proceed."

"Like what?"

"Actions that prove your loyalty to the Kings."

"Sure. I get it." Elijah leaned back, crossing his ankles.

Mikko mimicked his pose. "Kill Tia."

Elijah forced himself to remain nonchalant, though the order sucked the air from his lungs. He longed to tackle Mikko for even speaking such heinous words and Elijah infused every ounce of his self-control not to react to the demand. He snorted. "You said it yourself, she's a Fed. How am I supposed to get close enough to her to pull that off?"

"I'd say that's your problem. Be creative. But whatever you do, provide proof."

Elijah exhaled, mind whirling. "Fine."

"Good." Mikko rose to his feet. "Let me know when you've finished." Mikko's cell phone rang. A strange look crossed his face as he glanced down at the screen. Apprehension? He answered. "Yeah?"

A pause. Elijah couldn't hear the caller's voice, but Mikko's expression told him everything. Something big was about to go down, and the gang leader wasn't calling the shots.

"Got it. Yep. On my way." He pocketed the

phone. "Plans changed. It's go time." Mikko waved the gun. "Don't make me kill you."

Elijah tried not to show his relief. It was finally happening.

Now to tell the team.

SEVENTEEN

Tiandra sat in the BOO, staring at her cell phone, the Polaroid picture she'd found at the grain elevator on the screen.

"Still wondering if it's Penny?" Skyler placed a Styrofoam cup of coffee in front of her.

"Thanks." She wrapped her hands around the cup. "Yeah. The girl is familiar, and Penny lost her brother, Hank, when he was a teen."

"Hmm, here's something interesting," Eliana said, interrupting them. "I used the facial recognition software in PHACE," she said, referring to her phenotyping program. "And it pulled up the name John French from the DMV site." She typed furiously.

Skyler and Tiandra met each other's gazes.

"Now I'm really confused," Tiandra said.

"Oh," Eliana gasped. "There's more. John died of a gunshot wound sustained in an Omaha DEA raid in March 2001."

"That's the 03/01 from Graham's phone!" Skyler bolted to her feet and grabbed her laptop, tapping away at the keys.

"Did Penny lie about her name?" Tiandra asked. "Was it her brother?"

"That I can't say for sure," Eliana said. "I'll keep digging, but whoever managed the hospital video has tech skills. Penny's identity could be forged or stolen."

"If so, who's trying to silence her?" Skyler picked up her phone. "I'll check in on her security detail."

Tiandra's mind whirled. "Did Penny play me the entire time, knowing full well who Graham was? I need to talk to Elijah! He's walking into a trap!" She glanced at her watch. "I'm supposed to meet him in half an hour. I gotta go."

"Tiandra, let me go with you." Skyler stood.

"No. We can't risk being seen together." Tiandra shrugged into her winter coat, then leashed her K-9. "I'll find a way. Keep an eye on Penny."

"Maybe you should wait," Eliana said. "At least until Riker, Chance, and Walsh return."

"No, Bosco and I are cool. We got this." Tiandra gave a slight wave and hurried from the building.

Unsure what it all meant, Tiandra's instincts warned they were on the cusp of finding the answers, but she had to update Elijah. She loaded Bosco into the backseat. "We're close," she said to him, starting the engine.

She drove to Lovers Leap Trailhead to meet Elijah, praying she wasn't too late.

Tiandra maintained a steady pace, slower because of the icy winding street that took her to Badger Clark Road as she made her way through Custer State Park. She reached a bend when a set of headlights blared brightly, forcing her to avert her eyes. She glanced up to see the truck barreling straight for her. She had nowhere to turn. Images of her earlier accident raced to the forefront of her mind. Not again.

"Bosco, down!" she hollered, bracing for the hit.

The sound of metal on metal reverberated through the compact car and Tiandra's head whipped forward with the impact. A yelp from behind her drove a spear of fear into her heart. "Bosco." She said the word but never heard it. Had she spoken?

The sounds of men's voices drew closer. Tiandra reached for her gun.

Bullets pelted the vehicle, shattering the rear windshield. Tiandra dived to the side, glass raining on her from the windows.

Tiandra's task force cell phone chimed with a text message. Rapid gunfire continued all around her in an endless rendition. Forced to remain leaning over the console, hands covering her head, she cried, "Bosco, stay down!"

Then silence.

In the darkness, Tiandra prayed for her and Bosco's life. When the shots ceased, she sat up in the seat only to find the barrel of a gun aimed at her through the driver's window.

"Hello, Agent Daugherty," a familiar man's voice said.

"Mikko." Tiandra gasped.

"I've been waiting for you."

* * *

Elijah texted the address for the drug deal to the team. Then he added another message. Tell Tiandra not to meet me. Deal's going down.

Grateful for the interruption that stalled Mikko's ridiculous and impossible demand, Elijah prayed for wisdom. How was he supposed to prove he'd killed her? His hands gripped the steering wheel as concern, fear, and anxiety swarmed him. He sat waiting for Mikko to return. Had he made Elijah park in the dead-end spot as part of his sick games? His phone rang. Mikko. "Yeah?"

"Pick me up at 27887 26th Road. Now. I'll send coordinates by text."

"On my way." Elijah disconnected. The text pinged on his phone. This was it! He forwarded the information to the team on his task force cell phone before shifting into gear and driving to meet Mikko.

No reply from the team after ten minutes sent Elijah's worry into overdrive. Should he hold off? No, this was what they'd anticipated all this time. He lifted the phone and called Tiandra. It rang several times with no answer.

Elijah pulled onto 26th Road, noticing a house at the far end of the lane. He edged forward. The secluded home had lots of hardy shrubs and evergreens concealing the grounds. Was the task force nearby?

He hoped so.

Elijah parked beside Mikko's Mercedes.

He reached for his gun, then realized Mikko still had it. Great. Unarmed was the perfect way to handle this situation. He slid out from the driver's seat and surveyed the area. Quiet. Too quiet. Should return to the road and call the team again?

A light glowed from inside.

Elijah took a fortifying breath and walked up the porch steps and rapped twice on the ajar door before entering. "Mikko?"

The door slammed behind him, and Elijah spun. A woman stood in the shadows. "Drop to your knees," she ordered.

"Why would I do that?" Elijah countered. "Where's Mikko?"

"He'll be here soon," she answered, stepping forward and allowing Elijah to see her face. He recognized her from the hideout. The same woman who had told them the gang didn't appreciate their recent promotion. She held a gun aimed at him.

"I recognize you," he said.

"No, you don't," she replied. "But you knew my brother."

Elijah blinked.

She flipped on the overhead light, illuminating Tiandra bound and gagged on the floor where she sat, legs outstretched. Her ankles were free. Why hadn't Tiandra run? Something kept her complacent. Where was Bosco?

"Here's your cop friend."

Fury enveloped Elijah. "Who are you?"

"You haven't put it together yet?" She spat the question in a mocking tone. "Drop to your knees with your hands behind your head or I'll shoot her."

He did as she demanded.

"I'm going to bind you. Fight me and I'll kill her. Trust me when I say I don't have to be near her to do it," she warned. "You've seen my skills with fire and explosives. Don't test me."

Elijah swallowed hard as she moved with impressively quick speed, zip-tying his wrists and ankles. She left a small gap between his boots, no doubt intending to make him walk to another location.

She stepped back, positioned between him and Tiandra.

"So, you were the little girl in the picture?" Elijah asked. "Was that your big brother?"

"Ah, ringing bells in your dim brain, is it?" The woman tilted her head.

"Remind me. Who are you?"

"Nila French."

Elijah processed the name in his mind, unable to draw any connections.

"You don't remember!" She snorted, clearly agitated. "You destroy someone's family, kill an innocent teenager, and don't even have the courtesy to recall the names of those you murdered mercilessly."

Understanding hovered in Tiandra's expression,

implying she'd figured out what the woman ranted about. She must've discovered a clue when they'd parted and hadn't been able to share it with him. The same thing had happened with Graham, and the irony wasn't lost on him. He recalled the picture of the little girl with the teenager. Had Graham killed the boy? Was this connected to an old DEA case? "Did you know your brother was involved with gangs and drugs?" he asked, attempting to connect the dots.

Nila sighed. "I see. So that makes your crimes acceptable?" She tilted her head, sweeping a strand of dark blonde hair over her shoulder and jolting a memory for Elijah. "John was a child, in eleventh grade at Omaha Central high school!"

Elijah rifled through everything he'd learned in the investigation. The team had found a picture of Mikko with a woman. Was that Nila? Had Graham discovered her identity? Nila spoke as though she believed Elijah had killed her brother, but he'd never taken another person's life. Which meant Nila assumed he was Graham.

"Tell me about John."

"It's a little late now, isn't it?" Nila asked. "You and your vicious task force invaded that room, intending to destroy horrible criminals. When you didn't find them, you shot an innocent boy instead."

"He was dealing, involved with the gang," Elijah surmised.

"Don't justify your actions!" she bellowed.

"The saddest part is it only took one time for me to recognize you at the hideout. I will avenge my brother."

"Then why not just kill me?"

"Oh, it wasn't for lack of trying. You're like a cat, with all your extra lives." She laughed bitterly. "I thought running you off the road would've been enough. But the men I sent were incompetent. You dodged death at every turn with them. But this is so much better. Hands-on, face-to-face, is priceless. I get to watch you die."

"You were living at the elevator."

"Yeah, temporarily." She shrugged. "You two figured that out fast. Good job. Too late, and you lost, but you earned a star for effort."

The door swung open, and Mikko entered. "Honey, I'm home." He grinned. "And I see the gang's all here."

"You were in this together the whole time?" Elijah asked, determined to stall by keeping them talking. "What about Penny?"

Nila snorted. "She thought she'd blackmail Mikko into staying with her. We showed her."

A strange expression passed over Mikko's face. Did the man regret hurting Penny?

"It was going great until your girlfriend inter-rupted everything. Penny is like a cockroach. No matter how many times I tried to eliminate her, you interfered." Nila shook her head. "She'll never recover from the drugs I injected her with. At least not without my help."

Tiandra mumbled behind the gag and shook her head.

"It was you at the hospital?" Elijah asked, desperate to keep her talking until the task force arrived. "You impersonated Tiandra. But why?"

"Penny found out about us," Mikko replied. "She wouldn't walk away."

"Worse, she thought she'd tell the Kings and Locos about our little plan." Nila tsked. "That was her demise."

"But you're with the 29 Locos Cartel. You can't also be with Mikko in the Kings," Elijah said.

She nodded with a grin. "Not just one of the Locos. I will be the leader when I hand them the drugs the Kings get tonight."

"*We* will," Mikko corrected.

"Right, baby, we will," she assured him with a kiss to his cheek.

He smiled and turned to face Tiandra.

From the corner of his eye Elijah saw Nila withdraw a yellow object from her pocket and press it against Mikko's back. A spark and clicking sound emitted. Elijah recognized both. It was a Taser. A second later Mikko dropped to the floor, quivering.

Nila secured his wrists and ankles with zip-ties, leaving room around his boots for him to shuffle as she'd done with Elijah. "Not so fast, baby."

Tiandra and Elijah shared a stunned communication. Nila had just Tasered her boyfriend. Why?

"What're you doing?" Mikko gasped, his eyes wide as the voltage left his system.

"There can only be one leader," she said, shaking her head.

"We're partners. I did everything for you." Mikko struggled to sit up.

"I appreciate your efforts, but you're not trustworthy." Nila stood, a hand on her hip as though speaking to an insolent child. "You betrayed the Kings and poor Penny. Who's to say you wouldn't do the same to me? Mama always said never trust a cheater."

The woman was out of control. "Don't do this, Nila," Elijah pleaded. "You want revenge for John. I get that. Take it out on me. But let Tiandra go. She's done nothing to you."

"Did you send your team the address for the drug deal?" Nila asked, ignoring his request.

He gaped.

"Won't it be perfect when they arrive and find the Kings?" She laughed. "Two birds and all that. And your team will be too far away to help you. Aren't I brilliant?" She'd known the entire time he and Tiandra were undercover?

"Where is the real deal happening?" Mikko asked. "How did you know? They told you?"

Nila shrugged. "Let's just say I figured out a few things, baby. You made it easy. Thank you for that."

"I trusted you!" Mikko bellowed, stomping his bound feet on the hardwood floor.

"Well, that was part of the plan. Why else would you do everything I asked?"

Watching the dynamic between the two, though interesting, didn't provide Elijah the needed time. HFTF would arrive at the wrong location. The clock was ticking. Nila had made sure Elijah sent them on a useless chase, eliminating his and Tiandra's backup. They were on their own.

Mikko launched into a myriad of curses at Nila. "You sold me to buy your position with the 29 Locos!"

"I did," she agreed. "And now you've served your purpose and I need to clean house."

Elijah met Tiandra's eyes in a silent confirmation that Nila was the insider Graham had discovered.

"Please, Nila. I love you. I've given up everything to be with you," Mikko pleaded. The man's desperation oozed through his words.

"Thanks," she replied dismissively.

"All right, everyone, on your feet and move to the hallway." Nila gripped Tiandra's arm, the same one Elijah knew was injured in the accident, and wrenched it upward, causing Tiandra to wince and groan behind the gag.

"Graham, you lead the way," Nila said.

Elijah stiffened at his brother's name. He pushed himself to stand, and in the awkward walk he'd seen many convicts use in their restraints, complied with her demands, moving to the hallway.

"Go into the room to the right," Nila barked.

Elijah entered the room, focusing on the dog kennel positioned at the far side. Bosco slowly rose, teetering. She'd obviously drugged the poor Malinois, but he was alive.

"Sit down by the mutt," she instructed.

"Hey, buddy," Elijah reassured.

A cry from behind him indicated Tiandra was also relieved to see her partner.

The trio moved closer and dropped to the floor.

"I love you," Mikko pleaded. "Don't do this. You can trust me!"

"Now you sound pathetic," Nila spat at him. "Take it like a man, Michael!"

He silenced at the use of his real name.

Nila gestured to the wall where a clock hung, wires trailing from it. No doubt another one of her explosives. "This took longer than I anticipated. I really must go. You all enjoy your last—" she seemed to count the minutes "—three minutes together."

"Tell me!" Mikko cried. "Where is the deal happening!"

"Now see, sweetie, this is why I can't have you dragging me down. You never remember anything. Merry Christmas!" She winked and closed the door, the lock clicking with finality.

Elijah looked at Tiandra, leaning against the dog

kennel. This was it. Should he tell her he loved her with the few remaining moments of his life? No. He'd honor Graham by withholding his feelings for Tiandra. He'd failed in every way to protect her. He didn't solve the case or arrest his brother's assassin. The only thing left for him to do now was to die in silence, never confessing he'd fallen in love with Tiandra.

EIGHTEEN

Tiandra wriggled her fingers between the kennel bars. She couldn't speak the command, so she prayed Bosco would remember the trick they'd worked on a few times before the accident. In a soft reassurance Bosco's muzzle brushed her skin. Leaning to the side, she used the metal edges of the cage to pick at the gag. Finally, she pulled an edge free. The fabric was tight against her mouth, but the small win propelled her to continue until she'd tugged it off completely. Mikko had bound her with rope as opposed to Nila's use of zip-ties and she'd not bound her ankles. Both provided Tiandra the advantage.

With a deep inhale, she breathed air into her lungs. "Bosco, I need your help," she said. "Get the rope." She wriggled her fingers again. If he got hold of the cord binding her wrists and pulled, she might be able to get free.

"She used me," Mikko rambled. "She lied to me."

"Dude, shut up," Elijah snapped. "We have bigger problems."

Bosco gripped the cord and tugged. Tiandra leaned forward and heard the satisfying snap. The rope dropped off her wrists. "Good job!" She turned and quickly opened the latch on the kennel and the Malinois bounded into her arms. She hugged him, running her fingers through his soft fur.

Elijah gaped as she got to her feet. "How did you—"

"I'll tell you later." Tiandra searched for something to break off his bindings, glancing at the clock. She located a wrench on a shelf near the door. Tiandra placed the tool between the plastic and twisted. The zip-ties fell off.

"Me too!" Mikko cried.

"Not happening," Elijah said. "But we need to cut the one off his feet."

Tiandra used the tool to release Mikko's ankles, and together they helped him to stand. Tiandra glanced at her watch. "We have about forty seconds to get out of here."

"Is the bomb rigged to the door?" Elijah asked.

"No, I watched, and she didn't have any wires." Tiandra gripped the handle, twisting slowly. The door swung open, and they hurried from the room into the empty house.

Wordlessly, they sprinted outside, Mikko between them and Bosco beside her.

The Mercedes was gone but a second SUV sat parked.

"That's mine," Mikko said. "Keys are in it."

They rushed to the vehicle and loaded Bosco while Elijah shoved Mikko into the backseat with the dog.

"Guard," Tiandra ordered.

Bosco stood in position, emitting a low warning growl.

Mikko winced. "Good doggie."

Tiandra threw the SUV into Drive and sped from the property. They reached the corner of the road just as the bomb detonated.

"Notify the team," Tiandra said.

"If I help you, will you let me go?" Mikko asked.

"Um, no," Elijah answered.

"Your cell phone is tapped," Mikko said.

"Not this one." Elijah removed his task force device from his boot. He called Walsh and placed it on speakerphone. "Don't go to the location! It's a trap!" He launched into a rapid explanation.

"We figured that out when we got the weird text message from Tiandra," Eliana added. "It was missing her Bosco phrase."

Elijah glanced at Tiandra. "Later," she whispered.

"We'll make sure law enforcement arrests the Kings, but where is the deal taking place?" Walsh inserted, regaining the conversation.

"We're still working on that," Elijah said.

"I'll help if you give me an agreement," Mikko whined.

"Only if you provide the information," Walsh replied. "We're running out of time. Where?"

"We talked about buying a piece of land near Deadwood. It's gotta be there," Mikko said.

He provided directions, and Tiandra merged onto the highway, headed to the location.

"We'll meet you there," Walsh said.

"What phrase was Eliana talking about?" Elijah asked after the call had ended, keeping his voice low.

Tiandra turned on the radio, the music preventing Mikko from overhearing. "I always say 'Bosco and I are cool.' It's a code to prove I'm the sender of the message. Since that was missing, it triggered their suspicions."

"Have I mentioned how incredibly brilliant you are?" Elijah grinned.

"Don't let me stop you from saying it again," Tiandra teased.

The drive was lengthy and when they finally approached the property, Tiandra spotted several vehicles in a circle. She killed the lights, parking on a hill overlooking the area.

"Call Walsh," she said to Elijah.

"We're two minutes out," Walsh greeted and promptly disconnected.

She and Elijah shared a worried look. A lot could happen in two minutes.

Below, a van pulled up to the other vehicles and Nila slid out of the passenger seat, then walked toward a tall man.

"We can't wait." Tiandra twisted in her seat. "Where's your gun?"

Mikko frowned.

"Tell me!" Tiandra snapped.

"In the console," Mikko replied.

She withdrew the weapon. One pistol wasn't much against the criminals in the valley below, but they had no other option. "We have to go in."

"Yep." Elijah faced Mikko. "Stay here and don't do anything you'll regret."

"We're down a gun. We need Bosco," Tiandra said.

They exited the SUV and Tiandra released the dog and locked the doors with Mikko inside. She prayed he wouldn't escape. Slowly descending the hill to where the players assembled below, she kept her Glock at the ready as she mentally planned out their next move.

Before she could take action, she saw a line of SUVs swarm the area, coming in dark. Gazing farther down the road, she recognized the state patrol vehicles approaching.

"That was a fast two minutes," Elijah said on a relieved breath.

Shouts of "Get down!" and "Police!" filled the night air.

Several gang members tried escaping, ensuing chaos, with law enforcement descending on the fleeing criminals.

Movement in her peripheral vision caught Tiandra's attention. She turned to see Mikko bolting from the SUV. "Bosco, takedown."

The Malinois took off like a shot after Mikko.

The man looked over his shoulder and screamed.

Bosco closed the distance as Tiandra chased after them. "Stop or my dog will bite you," she hollered.

Mikko ignored her and continued running.

Bosco launched into the air and tackled Mikko to the ground. He growled, jaws clamped on Mikko's leg. The man's screams carried to Tiandra as she met them. "Get him off me! Help! Help!"

"Be still and shut up or he'll hold on!" she warned.

Mikko quieted and stopped fighting the dog.

"Release!" Tiandra ordered.

With a final growl, Bosco released his bite and stepped back in a slow, stalking, I-dare-you-to-move-again stance.

Skyler jogged to them and snapped handcuffs on Mikko, who was pleading excuses for his behavior.

Tiandra and Bosco returned to Elijah. He stood beside a patrol car with a handcuffed Nila. "It's in your best interest to cooperate," he warned her as she hung her head.

Nila shrugged.

"You've betrayed the 29 Locos Cartel and the Kings," Tiandra said, approaching. "Once that comes to light, you'll be on their kill list."

"Fine. I'll talk," Nila groused.

"Good, let's start with what you injected into Penny's IV line," Tiandra said.

Nila smirked. "Not here. I want a deal."

"Knock it off," Elijah snapped. "Tell us now."

"Without the specifics, she'll die," Nila taunted. "Give me reassurances."

"Boss." Tiandra waved at Walsh and sprinted to talk to him out of Nila's earshot.

"Okay," Walsh said, walking over to Nila. "This is simple. If Penny dies, the offer is gone. I'll make sure the authorities are aware of your cooperation. I'll also request leniency in your sentencing, since either way you're going away for an extended time." Walsh crossed his arms over his massive chest. "That's the best I can do."

Nila's face blanched with understanding. "Fine." She blurted the details for a recipe of chemicals new to Tiandra.

Walsh took notes and quickly made a call, repeating the information to someone on the other end of the line.

Still, Nila seemed determined to rationalize her actions. "John deserved justice," she argued.

"Your brother may or may not have chosen a different lifestyle, but your activities did nothing to honor him," Elijah said.

"You don't have a clue about honor!" she spat.

"Honoring someone you love means putting their needs above your own," Elijah said, his gaze meeting Tiandra's. "Your selfish ambition blew up in your face. Now, all you'll have is a lifetime in prison."

"Merry Christmas to me," Nila grumbled.

"I'll handle her." Walsh smiled, pocketing his phone and returning to the conversation. "You two get to Graham. There's great news."

Nila did a double take, clearly confused, but nobody bothered to tell her the truth about Elijah's identity.

Tiandra and Elijah sprinted toward the closest HFTF vehicle where Skyler stood waiting. "I'll drive you."

"Is there a plane?" Elijah asked as they loaded into the SUV. How else would they get to the Florida hospital where they'd seen Graham?

"Nope," Skyler said, "Graham's in Rapid City."

"B-But—" Elijah stammered.

"We had him transferred a while back," Skyler explained.

They made the short commute to the hospital with Eliana on speakerphone to provide the update.

"Graham's condition is improving," she expounded. "He's awake, alert and ready for company."

"What a wonderful Christmas day surprise!" Tiandra squeezed Elijah's hand. Her throat thickened with emotion. Confessing her feelings wasn't acceptable. Not now. He deserved to reconcile with Graham, and she had no right to interfere in that. But with all her heart, she wanted to tell Elijah she'd fallen in love with him.

Christmas was a time for healing. The perfect opportunity for her to make her own reconciliations. Tiandra glanced at her cell phone and typed a message to Meghan.

I miss you. Let's talk soon.

Her sister's reply came almost instantaneously. I can't wait. I love you.

Elijah strode into the hospital, his heart pumping triple time. This was it.

He entered Graham's room and exhaled with relief at the sight of his brother sitting up in bed. He looked pale and banged up, but he was alive.

"Hey!" Graham smiled widely. "Did you bring food?"

Elijah chuckled and rushed forward, embracing his twin.

They stayed that way for several seconds before Graham laughed. "Okay, now it's just weird."

Elijah stepped back and dragged a chair beside the bed.

"Eliana said I've missed a lot," Graham began.

"You have no idea." Elijah launched into the explanation of the events, narrowly dodging his attraction to Tiandra. "It was quite an experience."

"Thank you," Graham said. "I'd still be in danger without your help."

Elijah shrugged. "No big deal."

"How did you like working with the team?" Graham shifted on the bed, wincing. "It's hard to get comfortable."

His brother's condition had improved, but his casted arm and leg would take time to heal. "I'm sorry you're stuck there."

"No sweat. Nurses think I'm cute here," he laughed. "Was Tiandra a good partner?"

At the mention of her name, Elijah's throat tightened, and he averted Graham's gaze. "They're all wonderful."

"For real. Once you're in, you never want to leave the group." Graham tilted his head. "Why are you staring at me with that weird expression? What's wrong?"

"I'm just glad you're okay." Elijah shrugged. "I learned a ton. Tiandra was amazing. Bosco too."

"They're the dream team."

"I got a little reminder in the importance of telling people how we feel."

"I couldn't agree more."

"You're my brother and I love you." Elijah leaned forward, his elbows resting on his knees. "Whatever happened between us, it's gone, okay? New beginnings."

"Amen." Graham smiled.

"I resented you," Elijah blurted.

Graham rolled his eyes. "Duh."

"You knew?"

"Bro, we're twins. I have the inside track on you 24/7."

"But you never said anything."

"Nell rocked your boat. She hurt you," Graham said.

"Yeah, but that wasn't your fault, even though I blamed you." Elijah glanced down. "I hated being in your shadow. Always feeling inferior."

"That's all in your head. You're everything I want to be."

Elijah blinked. "What?"

"For real. You maintain your cool no matter what. That's skill." Graham met his eyes. "Nell was the catalyst for our issues. But you're my brother. I'd never jeopardize that relationship."

"Can you ever forgive me?"

"Dude, there's nothing to forgive."

Elijah stood and hugged Graham again.

"Okay, we gotta stop that." Graham laughed. "But I'd like to know you as a friend."

"Me too." Elijah dropped into the seat.

"You're right, though. I need to man up and talk about my feelings. This whole life-threatening thing taught me there might not be a second chance." Graham shifted in the bed. "Remember the woman I talked about?"

Images of Tiandra bounced to Elijah's mind. "Yeah."

"I get tongue-tied around her."

"You?" Elijah blinked. "G, that's unbelievable."

"Right? I mean, that's why I'm certain she's the one. I never struggle talking to women."

"Yes, I'm aware." Elijah rolled his eyes.

"So, you'll do me a solid?"

"What? Teach you how to be awkward like me?" Elijah joked.

"No, for real, bro. I need help."

Elijah braced. This was it. Graham would tell Tiandra he was in love with her, and she'd fall into his arms. "Of course."

"Maybe you could get her to come here." Graham shook his head. "Wait. Don't want to play the I'm-in-a-hospital-bed-so-you-can't-say-no card."

"You're killing me here."

"How do I approach her?"

"Just be honest."

"Right." Graham nodded. "Lay it all out there and hope for the best."

Elijah recalled how Tiandra had said she didn't share Graham's feelings. He wouldn't set up his brother to get hurt, but how could he betray her trust? "Except whatever happens, the right woman is out there."

Graham quirked a brow. "What're you saying? Do you know Deputy Audrey Simpson?"

"Who?" Confused, Elijah asked, "What's she got to do with anything?"

"Bro, she's the one. She works for the Keystone County Sheriff. I've been trying to work up the guts to ask her out for months."

"What?" Elijah blinked. "What about Tiandra?"

As soon as her name escaped his lips, Elijah's face warmed.

"Tiandra?" This time, Graham blinked. "What about her?"

"You're not in love with her?"

His brother burst out laughing. "Um. No. Is that why you got all weird just now?"

"I wasn't weird. I...thought you had a thing for her."

"Dude, you're so in love with her you can't even say her name without oozing heart bubbles."

Elijah laughed.

"Tiandra is amazing. Brilliant and gorgeous." Graham smiled. "But no, we're only friends. She's like a sister. That's why I didn't want her involved in the case. I was worried Nila would go after her."

"I was sure you were trying to protect her." Elijah exhaled. "I can't tell you what a relief that is."

"So, ask her out," Graham said, leaning forward as much as his injuries permitted. "With my blessing."

"Except I'm not interested in dating her. She's the one. I want to marry her."

Graham blinked, a wide smile spreading over his face. "Outstanding!"

A rap on the door interrupted them as the rest of the team entered.

"He's back!" Riker cheered.

"'Bout time, slacker," Skyler teased.

"Finally!" Chance said.

In a round of hugs and happy encouragement, Elijah slipped from the room, allowing the group to reunite. Walsh stopped him in the hallway. "You did an terrific job on this case."

"Thank you, sir," Elijah said.

"It just so happens, we have an opening on our team," Walsh said. "No pressure. Offer is there if you'd like."

"All due respect—" Elijah began, then remembering Walsh hated the phrase, corrected, "I should probably talk with Graham about it."

"He's the one who suggested it," Tiandra said from behind him.

Elijah spun to face her. "Oh. Well. Thank you, I'll think it over."

"Excellent." He walked past them, whistling.

"It's so great to see Graham back to himself," Tiandra said.

"Definitely." Elijah shoved his hands into his pockets. "Take a walk with me? I discovered some new information."

"You have my undivided attention."

They strolled to the elevators and Elijah pressed the down button. "My brother used his current status to guilt Walsh into giving me a job offer." The familiar sting of being in Graham's shadow threatened again.

"Didn't you learn anything while working with us?" Tiandra paused, tilting her head. "Walsh doesn't function under compulsion. If he offered you a position, it's based purely on his confidence in your abilities."

Elijah digested that information. "He isn't obligated?"

"Um, no." Tiandra took his hand. "You've proven yourself a great warrior, Elijah. The team wants you to join us. If you'd stuck around when the cavalry came bursting in, they'd have told you themselves."

The doors opened and they entered the elevator. Elijah pressed the number one button.

"This is much better than a grain elevator."

He chuckled, feeling freer and happier than he had in months.

They exited on the main floor and strode along where bright Christmas lights and garland decorated the hallway.

Could he really be a part of the elite Heartland Fugitive Task Force? The idea sent a wave of excitement coursing through him.

"On a personal note, I think you'd be an amazing team member."

"Thank you," he whispered, then redirecting said, "So, um, I talked to Graham about his feelings for you."

"You did?" Tiandra winced. "I have to address that."

"Yeah, don't. Turns out I totally misread him. He's got a thing for Deputy Audrey Simpson."

"I'm not sure if I'm relieved or hurt." Tiandra

chuckled. "Just kidding. Come to think of it, I remember him getting skittish whenever she was around. That's out of character for him." She put a finger to her lips. "And, if memory serves me correctly, she also had a little twinkle in her eye when she was around him."

"Yep. That's the woman he's in love with." Elijah shoved his hands into his pockets again. "I have fought everything within me not to tell you."

He pulled Tiandra to the side, and they sat in an alcove surrounded by plants. A Christmas tree stood in the corner tastefully adorned in rose gold ornaments and tinsel.

"About what?" Tiandra asked.

"When Nila had us in the house, I realized she still believed I was Graham. It was the last chance to make things right with my brother. I could take his place and let Nila think she'd won. Then he'd be safe."

Tiandra nodded. "I figured that out when you didn't correct her."

"But all I wanted to do just before Bosco got your bindings off—which by the way, I still gotta hear the story on that one—was to tell you…" He sucked in a breath and gripped both of Tiandra's hands into his own. "Whew. Okay, let me try that again. Now I can freely confess that you're the woman I'm in love with."

Tiandra's eyes shimmered. "I am? You are?"

"Head over boots," Elijah said.

"Same here." She grinned. "I'm glad you said it first, though."

Elijah blinked. "Really?"

"Yes. I just needed the right time to tell you I'd fallen in love with you."

"Me too." Elijah swallowed. "That's not entirely true. I didn't want to interfere with you and Graham."

Tiandra laughed. "Well, apparently that was never an issue."

"I know!"

"I'm glad I'm not the only one who fell hard." Her hazel eyes soaked him in.

He leaned closer, gently lifting her chin with a single fingertip, and brushed his lips against hers. The softness and sweet taste of her had him deepening the kiss. Tiandra melted into his embrace, and he held her tighter.

"Merry Christmas to us," he said, when they'd parted. He gestured overhead to the mistletoe hanging above them.

"One of many," she whispered.

"Tiandra Daugherty, I'd marry you today if you agreed. I hear the hospital has a nice chapel."

She laughed and winked. "If we don't invite my family, they'll kill me."

"Call them and get them on a plane." Elijah laughed. "Is tomorrow too soon for a wedding?"

She giggled. "Not soon enough."

* * * * *

*If you enjoyed this story, look for these
other books by Sharee Stover:*

Cold Case Trail
Tracking Concealed Evidence
Framing the Marshal

Dear Reader,

Thank you for sharing in the story of Tiandra, K-9 Bosco and Elijah. I am so grateful for the time you took to spend with us!

One of my favorite quotes is something Tiandra considers in the story: "Soldiers are made. Warriors are born."

I have enjoyed writing the Heartland Fugitive Task Force series and especially have loved adding new characters to the team. I hope their adventures kept you on the edge of your seat!

I love hearing from readers. Please visit my website at www.shareestover.com and join my newsletter for the most up-to-date information on my books.

Blessings to you,
Sharee